Slowly l

She wondere
in the way he
need to step b

He smiled at he
then used a fore
you," he said, and
on her lips.

Abby sighed, wanting to grab him and draw him close, but knowing instinctively that would be the wrong thing to do. For both of them. A night of romantic play wouldn't resolve anything for either of them. In fact, it might only complicate matters. Man, she hated being sensible right then.

"Good night." Then he was gone.

A few minutes later she heard quiet music issuing from the living room piano. Much more peaceful than earlier. Maybe even a bit happy?

But no, she hadn't done anything to make him happy. No point in deluding herself. Too many clouds hung over his head.

* * *

Conard County: The Next Generation

A COWBOY FOR CHRISTMAS

BY
RACHEL LEE

MILLS
BOON

Published in Great Britain 2015
by Mills & Boon, an imprint of Harlequin (UK) Limited,
Eton House, 18-24 Paradise Road, Richmond, Surrey, TW9 1SR

© 2015 Susan Civil Brown

ISBN: 978-0-263-25186-9

23-1115

Harlequin (UK) Limited's policy is to use papers that are natural, renewable and recyclable products and made from wood grown in sustainable forests. The logging and manufacturing processes conform to the legal environmental regulations of the country of origin.

Printed and bound in Spain
by CPI, Barcelona

Rachel Lee was hooked on writing by the age of twelve and practiced her craft as she moved from place to place all over the United States. This *New York Times* bestselling author now resides in Florida and has the joy of writing full-time.

Chapter One

From the outside, the ranch house appeared ordinary. Large, from the days of big families, sided with freshly painted white clapboard, with a wide front porch. Inside, the house was anything but ordinary. It looked as if it might have come out of the pages of an interior design magazine.

With Christmas still ten weeks away, at least Abby didn't have to deal with decorations. And by Christmas, she hoped to have better plans for her future than this.

Abby had spent more than a week cleaning the house, erasing the last detritus of the remodeling, removing dust from every nook and cranny, making sure polished wood gleamed and mirrors provided perfect reflections.

It had been a lot of work, and she was certain she'd

used some muscles she hadn't needed in a while, but at last the house was ready for its new resident.

She wasn't.

She'd never met her employer. Being hired by someone who worked for Rory McLane had been unusual for her, but probably not for him. He was a big country music star, after all, and could probably afford people to do everything for him, maybe even dress him.

The thought made her giggle, easing a bit of her tension as she waited for her new boss to arrive. She certainly had little enough to giggle about these days.

She didn't mind the hard work at all. In fact, she'd enjoyed it. Not many jobs provided such a sense of accomplishment that she could actually see. What she minded were the circumstances that brought her here.

And she was uneasy about Rory McLane. With all his fame and money, he was probably puffed up and demanding. Egotistical. She clenched her fists for a moment and reminded herself that it didn't matter what he was like. She had to put up with it because the alternative was unthinkable. Her husband had run away with her former boss, leaving her jobless and then essentially homeless when he'd sold his family house. Whatever McLane was like, she had to endure it.

Behind the house was a barn that had been refurbished, too, turned into a recording studio that she had only glimpsed. A special crew had been sent in to set that up and clean it. She guessed it required an expertise no housekeeper with a dust rag and mop could provide.

All of it blew her away when she thought about it.

She reached out now and touched expensive woods no one around here could afford. She had stepped into a barn that housed not only a top-of-the-line recording studio but a kitchenette and a sitting area. She wondered if McLane might spend most of his time out there.

She hoped so, because she didn't expect to like him. She couldn't imagine how having all that money, all that success and all that adulation could fail to go to a person's head.

She saw dust down the driveway and realized he must be arriving. She'd heard he was flying in his own small plane, but she had no idea if he was coming alone. She half expected to see a stretch limo come up the drive, but instead there was nothing but a brand-new beige pickup truck.

One of the neighbors, maybe?

She drew closer to the front window and watched. Just one truck. And when it pulled to a halt in front of the porch, just one man climbed out.

Abby didn't follow celebrities, but curiosity had led her to look up Rory McLane on one of the multiple computers scattered throughout the house, and there was no mistaking the man who climbed out of the driver's seat.

Tall, lanky, wearing jeans, a blue shirt and well-worn cowboy boots. Dark hair a bit on the shaggy side. He turned and pulled out a cowboy hat that didn't look like any of the ones in his photos. This one had seen some mileage. He clapped it on his head.

This was not what she expected from his publicity photos. Instead of looking like a star, he looked like any rancher coming home.

No entourage. No gorgeous beauties, no stream of people. Just him, looking like an ordinary resident of this county.

Then he walked easily around the truck, dropped the tailgate and pulled out a couple of heavy suitcases. She watched, her mouth growing drier as he brought them up to the porch. Then he went back to the truck and pulled out a guitar case.

Nothing, absolutely nothing, had prepared her for the impact of this man in real life. His face looked a little careworn, but he was built like a stud. Broad shoulders, narrow hips, strong chin, straight nose… and when he looked toward the window he did it with eyes as blue as the Wyoming sky.

She could have stared at him forever. Odd, because he wasn't perfect. His attractiveness ran deeper than looks.

The guitar case hit the porch with a quiet thud, shaking her out of her preoccupation. He went back to close the tailgate, and she decided it was time to start her job. Such as opening the door for him?

Dreading the first encounter, she walked out into the large foyer and depressed the brass latch, opening the door wide just as he was climbing the porch steps again.

"Mr. McLane?" she queried, as if she didn't know. She wasn't going to give him the satisfaction of her instant recognition.

He smiled faintly. "You must be Abby Jason?"

"Yes, sir."

He paused just as he was about to lift one of the suitcases. Straightening, he put one hand on his narrow hips and studied her. She could imagine what he was seeing: corn-fed farm girl, a little too plump, plain, no makeup, work clothes. She hadn't dressed to impress.

"Do me a favor," he said, his voice a baritone that immediately suggested he'd be a great singer. "First names, and no sirs. I'm Rory. Nice to meet you, Abby. Are your rooms okay?"

"Very nice," she admitted. She hadn't expected to have her own small suite of rooms at the back of the house. Nicely furnished, too.

"Good. I'd love some coffee if that's not too much trouble. Just let me carry my bags in. I should be able to find my room since I approved the layout."

He said that with a kind of humor that surprised her. She managed a nod. "Coffee coming up."

"Staff of life," he said pleasantly. One heavy suit-case in each hand, he started past her.

She hesitated. "Should I bring the guitar inside the door?"

He paused. "Thanks. That's my old baby."

"Old baby?"

"My very first guitar. Nothing can replace it. Just set it in here, please."

She grabbed the case, put it in the foyer, closed the door and headed to the most modern kitchen she'd ever seen. Everything gleamed in stainless steel, the kind of kitchen a chef would want. Abby was no trained chef, just an ordinary everyday cook, but over the last week she had come to appreciate the ease of cleaning, if not the ease of removing smudges.

She'd had to read the directions on the coffee-maker, since it did everything except dance, but she'd mastered it. A thought struck her and she ran to the foot of the stairs. "Regular coffee or espresso?" she called up.

"Regular. Just black and strong."

The machine ground its own beans and measured out the water according to the number of cups she chose. Since she had no idea how much coffee he might want, she selected the strongest brew and hit the button for eight cups. At once the beans started to grind, the loudest sound in this house usually. Then the grinder stopped and the coffee began to drip.

Well, she thought with a rare burst of humor, at least she couldn't screw up the coffee.

Rory returned a few minutes later. Abby stood leaning against the counter, unsure of protocol. Would he be offended if she was sitting at the table when he entered? How would she know? She'd never dealt with the rich and famous before.

He strode into the room. She at once reached for a mug, but he stopped her. "Grab a seat. I can pour for myself, believe it or not. You want some?"

"Please," she said quietly, because any other answer might have seemed rude, and sank nervously into a seat at the kitchen table, a very nice creation of wood and a tile top with some kind of Native American pattern.

To her surprise, he brought two cups over and sat across from her.

"Quit looking so nervous," he said. "I never bit an employee yet."

Again she managed an uncertain smile. So far he'd been okay. She kept waiting for the other shoe to drop.

"I don't know what my manager told you when he hired you."

"Very little. I'm to cook and clean, I get one day off and whatever other time you choose to give me."

He nodded. "You'll get more than one day off. I'm not exactly incapable of looking after myself. Okay, ground rules."

She tensed.

"I came here to be alone. Since I'm considered an artist, I get to call it my reclusive period."

At that she felt another smile flicker over her face.

"Anyway, I really *do* want to be alone. I need some time away, time to work and find my voice again. I'm not looking for sympathy, just solitude. Get the creative juices going again. So don't expect me to have a lot of guests. In fact, I plan to avoid that as much as possible, although I'll probably get stalked by my agent and manager."

Abby blinked. "Why would they stalk you?"

"They make money when I'm touring. This is not making them money. They're also worried that my career might wind down if I stay away too long."

"Oh." She looked down. "A little mercenary?"

"In all of our interests. I'm not really criticizing, just warning you. They may show up even though I told them not to. Other than that, I'm not expecting anyone. But that doesn't mean I want to cut you off from everyone, so if you want to have friends over, well, you've got your own space, okay?"

She thought that was generous of him, considering he'd just told her he wanted solitude. "Thank you."

He nodded, took a long draft of coffee. "I'm not easy."

At that point she stiffened, sure she was about to meet the arrogance she expected.

"I keep weird hours when I'm composing. You can't plan meals around me. I may wander out to the studio and not be seen again for days. I realize that makes it tough on you, but if you can just make sure there's stuff in the fridge I can heat in the microwave or oven, we'll be fine. I might occasionally want to eat like a human being, but if so I'll let you know in advance. As for the groceries…" He shrugged. "I'm not a picky eater. If I want something in particular, I'll put it on a list. You got your housekeeping account, right?"

"Yes, your manager took care of that."

"If it's not enough, let me know. Money is one thing we won't have to worry about around here. If something breaks, feel free to call a repairman."

Relief was so great she felt a little bubble of unexpected laughter rise and escape her. It had been so long since she had wanted to laugh, it felt strange. "So wrap you in cotton wool?"

At that he flashed a grin. "Just pretend I'm a bear in a cage out there. Throw in some meat once in a while."

At that she laughed outright. "I think I get it."

"I may get a little more sociable as time passes, but right now…" He trailed off and his blue eyes stared somewhere beyond the room. "Back in Nashville, getting enough downtime is impossible. So call me the recluse of Conard County."

His gaze focused on her again. "You must have been a tot when I left twenty years ago."

"I think I was five or six."

"Couldn't wait to shake the dust of this place off

my heels," he admitted. "Look at me now. Like a pig headed back for my wallow."

She drew a breath and dared to ask, "Why?"

He tilted his head. "Some things can wear out your soul, Abby. Mine is worn to rags. I don't even enjoy my music anymore. That's got to change."

"You think being here can do that?"

"It built me. Maybe it can rebuild me." He sighed. "Guess I'm going to find out."

He rose and refilled his mug. "No calls. I have a private line and only three people have the house number. Any other calls, just say I'm unavailable and take a message, okay?"

"I can do that."

"I'm sure you can." Then he hesitated. "Guess I should give you my cell number, too, just in case. If you stumble on the stairs and break a leg, it might be a long time before you see me. Do you have a cell that works out here?"

She shook her head.

"Get one next time you're in town. And use your free time however you want. I don't expect you to be making busy work to fill the hours, and I don't expect you to be at my beck and call all the time."

Finally curiosity overwhelmed caution. "What exactly do you need a full-time housekeeper for?" A dangerous question considering she needed the job.

"For all the stuff I let slide when I'm composing. That'll be plenty." He winked. "You get to be my buffer against the real world. I'm hoping to be spending most of my time with my Muse. She's a demanding mistress."

He rinsed out his mug at the sink, and put it in the

brand-new dishwasher. "This is my hermitage and I'm the monk," he said, facing her. "Just think of it that way. And right now I'm going to go take a walk and see what the wind whispers to me."

His booted feet crunched on the desiccated grass of late summer and early autumn. A dry breeze blew steadily. Nashville was greener and more humid, and certainly warmer right now. As he strode out across fields covered with deep, dying grass and occasional tumbleweed, with nothing to block his view in most directions until his gaze ran up against the nearby mountains, he realized just how much he had missed Conard County.

It didn't take him long to reconnect with the youth who had felt this place was parching his soul. Well, over the years he'd found other ways to parch it. Maybe worse ways.

Long summer afternoons came back to him, when he'd been done with his chores and had hiked out to a quiet place where he could rest his back against a cottonwood and make up his songs with his battered guitar. Hours spent lying on his back looking up at occasional wisps of cloud against a painfully blue sky, listening for whatever whispered to him.

Long winters, frigid cold, when escape had been impossible unless he sat out in the barn with the horses, freezing his fingers until he couldn't feel the guitar strings anymore.

Surprisingly, he found himself actually looking forward to the winter that was right around the corner. He doubted his manager or anyone else would try to come out here then. By Christmas, maybe they'd accept that he was determined to stay here as long as he felt he needed it.

The breeze gusted a little, and he clapped his hand to his head to keep his hat from blowing away. The same hat he'd been wearing when he left here. Like some kind of talisman. He wondered if he was becoming superstitious.

Over the years, he'd realized how important it was to have creative friends. They'd spurred him on, creating a synergy that had benefitted them all. So what the hell had convinced him he needed to be all by himself again?

He couldn't reclaim the freshness and optimism of the kid who had left here. Too much had happened over the years. Yet deep inside he felt there was something buried that couldn't make its way out unless he provided the utter quiet and solitude it needed to be heard. Listening for voices on the wind seemed like a good enough place to start.

Cowboy boots weren't made for walking, even well-worn ones, and finally he decided he'd better head back. To what, he still didn't know.

The housekeeper, Abby, had sure caught his attention. He wondered when was the last time he'd seen a woman her age without a smidgen of makeup. Not that she needed any. Cute figure, too, from what he could tell under that loose work shirt she wore. A little plumper than he was used to from a town where everyone seemed to be trying to lose another ten pounds to compensate for the camera. He liked that plumpness. A man could cuddle up to those curves. He liked her long naturally brown hair, too, so carelessly caught up in a clip on the back of her head. It looked silky, begging for a touch. And her golden eyes reminded him of amber.

What he hadn't liked was the weariness he saw in her. A sorrow that touched her golden eyes and full lips. The way her smile and her laughter didn't come easily. Seemed as if they both needed some time to cure themselves.

He was curious about her, but stepped down on it. He hadn't come out here to make new friends or get tangled up in anything. No, he'd come to find his own footing and get his own head and heart sorted out.

Sometimes he felt as if he was dancing all the time to some insane piper. He needed a breather, some downtime, an escape from a pace that never really flagged. Oh, he could get some time by himself, but never enough of it. There was always something he needed to do, friends who wanted to get together…in short a full life. Too full. With one great big gaping hole in it, dug by his ex-wife Stella and her winning custody of their daughter, Regina.

He guessed he had some holes to patch, too. Being shed of Stella was a relief. He just wished the courts hadn't sided with her when she insisted a young girl needed her mother, not her father. He hadn't expected that, and regret still dogged him. That was killing him.

So maybe Brian, his manager, was right when he said Rory was running away. But running away had served him once before, and it might again. If it didn't, he could head back to Nashville in a few months and pick up the rat race again.

But the hollowness had been filling him for a while, and going through the motions wasn't the kind of life he wanted. He needed to find his music again, the music that had given him meaning and purpose. If he didn't, then he was nothing but a sham any longer.

He paused, listening to the wind. It had a music of its own, and once it had filled him with creative impulses. But after a few minutes, he gave up. He heard nothing in its sigh, not yet. Maybe he'd lost the ears to hear.

Abby watched his return, and wondered what to do. She'd made a lasagna that morning, figuring she could heat it whenever he was ready to eat, but Rory McLane had told her he'd eat whenever he felt like it. So what was she supposed to do?

He'd basically left her free to do as she liked, but maybe he didn't realize how difficult that might be for her. She was acutely aware that she was being paid generously, and felt as if she ought to be earning that check. Part of her job was feeding the man. A man who apparently didn't want to be fed, at least not on any kind of routine.

Awkward, that's what it was. Finally, deciding that she needed her supper even if he didn't, she popped the lasagna in the oven. She was going to take a small portion for herself, then section it up into individual servings either one of them could heat easily. It was the only way she could think to handle it.

She knew she had to try this his way, but she wondered if sooner or later they were going to need to have a more detailed talk about her role. Winging it might work for him, but already she had a million questions about how to best handle things for him.

She heard him come through the front door, and managed to put a note of cheer in her voice. "I just put a lasagna in the oven. Ready in about an hour if you decide you want to eat."

She heard his steps stop in the hallway and tensed, wondering if he'd remind her yet again that he didn't want to be bothered with anything.

Then she heard his approach. He stopped in the kitchen doorway. Easy to see how this man had become a heartthrob for millions. Her heart accelerated of its own accord, and she felt the first stirring of long-absent desire. Not good.

"Lasagna?" he said.

"Yes."

"Sounds good. I may…"

She heard a phone beep and he fell silent as he pulled a cell from his pocket. "Stella," he said with distaste. "Sorry. Give me a minute."

He walked out, leaving her alone in the kitchen again. For a guy who didn't want to be bothered, he was being bothered rather soon. She seemed to recall from her brief research on him that Stella was his ex. She still called him? Her own ex, Porter, hadn't spared a word for her since the divorce.

Fifteen minutes passed. She considered bringing out the salad she had prepared earlier, then decided it was too soon. Should she set places for both of them in here? Or maybe he'd want to eat alone in his fancy dining room.

Dang, there seemed to be more questions than answers with this job. He made it sound so easy, but as she was rapidly discovering a lack of guidance was anything but easy.

At long last she heard the unmistakable steps of his boots.

"Well," he said, "your job just got more complicated."

She whirled to look at him. "Yes?"

"That was my ex. I'll be leaving tomorrow to go pick up my daughter. It seems she's too much for Stella."

Abby could barely keep herself from gaping. "Too much?"

"Running off nannies constantly. Stella's too busy to deal with it." Rory astonished her with a big smile. "Hot damn," he said. "I'm getting my daughter! And not just for Christmas."

Abby felt her heart sink and the early stirrings of panic even as she appreciated the joy reflected in his smile. And what a smile it was, nearly depriving her of breath. The guy was clearly thrilled about seeing his daughter. That should have touched her.

Instead, the gnawing worry about how to handle this inchoate job burst out of her before she knew the words were coming. "I wasn't hired to be a babysitter."

His smile faded a bit. "I'm not asking you to. Regina's ten. I'm her father. Let me do my job and you do yours." Then he turned and left. Moments later she heard him head out the back door.

She hurried back to her suite and saw him walking toward the barn.

"Idiot," she said aloud to herself. What had possessed her to say that when the man was so clearly thrilled? What kind of selfish shrew was she becoming?

But a girl who was driving away her nannies?

All of a sudden this job seemed more complicated that she could have begun to imagine.

Chapter Two

Abby didn't see Rory again before he left the following morning. She tried to tell herself he was just being the hermit he had warned her he was going to be, but guilt rode her hard anyway. This was his house, and she'd had the nerve to let him know that she wasn't thrilled about the arrival of his daughter.

She'd be lucky if he didn't fire her when he got back. But the truth was, she hadn't been hired to be a babysitter, she knew next to nothing about kids and a troubled one would be more than she could adequately handle. Maybe she should have waited to bring it up, but concern had pushed the words out of her mouth at the worst possible time.

She wanted to bang her head on something. Porter's cheating and desertion weren't that far in the past, and she often felt she was turning into a person she didn't know and one she didn't especially like. Bitterness rose often, anger even more often, and resentment was one big mountain inside her.

Maybe worst of all was feeling like an utter failure. She hadn't been woman enough to keep a husband for two whole years. That meant there was something wrong with her. Right?

Fear, betrayal, failure—they'd become her constant companions. Now she had proved how they were twisting her by reacting to her boss's joy about his daughter with the most selfish response she could have voiced.

Maybe this wasn't a new version of her. Maybe this was what she had been all along without realizing it. If she'd been treating Porter the way she had treated Rory, why wouldn't he leave her?

Everything inside her felt so miserably mixed up she couldn't figure out up and down anymore. That certainly made her incapable of looking after a child, but she could have been more diplomatic.

Frustrated with herself, she cleaned the whole house again. There were four elaborate guest rooms upstairs, each with its own color theme, but no way to figure out which one Regina might get. Nothing she could do about that.

She peeked into the master suite, a bright sunny room decorated in blues and browns that indelibly stamped it as masculine. She dusted it thoroughly, cleaned the bathroom until it shone, changed the sheets, then left the sanctuary otherwise untouched.

She drove into town to the library to get some books to read, then found herself unable to concentrate on them. She'd done something stupid, and she wasn't going to know the outcome until Rory returned. If she had a chance, she ought to apologize. Not for refusing to be a babysitter. She knew she wasn't adequate for that. But for the way she had said it. For her timing.

Except the truth stared her in the face. She *hadn't* been hired to care for a child, and if that had been mentioned before she accepted the position, she might have looked for something else. As if jobs grew on trees.

She groaned, being honest with herself. Working at the truck stop hadn't been quite enough to meet her bills, and soon she would have had no place to go. This job was an unexpected godsend.

She didn't have anything against kids. It was just that she didn't feel adequate to taking care of one, beyond maybe cooking and cleaning. She'd never had a younger sister or brother to practice on. She'd never babysat anybody, because she'd always had a job after school. Inadequate, that was what she was, but why should that surprise her?

On the other hand, she knew perfectly well she couldn't find another job that paid as well as this one. A generous salary with room and board included. If she could hang on for a year, she'd be able to save enough to resume her college education.

But instead of thinking of that, she'd had an utterly selfish and ugly reaction to a man's joy. Job or no job, she needed to straighten that out as soon as he came back.

Two days later the hour of her reckoning arrived. Rory called, saying they were at the airport but were going to stop at the grocery. Did she need anything?

A polite, courteous call, utterly unnecessary. She didn't know how to judge this man at all. "I'm fine. Just whatever you and Regina need."

"Okay. I hope you don't have a problem with dogs."

"Dogs?"

"Regina brought her Great Dane with her. Thank goodness he's a good flier is all I have to say."

"A Great Dane?" She almost squeaked.

"Yup. I figure I need to buy all the dog food at the feed store before we come back." Then he surprised her with a laugh. "Don't panic, he's a gentle giant."

A dog and a kid. After hanging up the phone, Abby sat at the table. A *huge* dog and a troublesome kid. Oh, this could get interesting.

A couple of hours later, she found out. The truck pulled up and almost instantly a coltish girl with her father's dark hair and blue eyes bounded out of the passenger side, and right after came a dog that was bigger than she was. A Harlequin Great Dane, Abby guessed, given that he was white with black spots. Beautiful.

Big.

Regina went tearing off over the open landscape, the dog racing along with her. Rory stood watching for a minute, then went to the back of the truck and began unloading.

Abby decided there'd never be a better time to apologize to him, so she hurried out. "Can I help?" she asked.

"Groceries, if you don't mind. Apparently certain foods are necessary to the survival of ten-year-olds. As for the dog food, unless you want to heft forty-pound sacks, leave that to me. I guess I can keep them out in the barn."

"Didn't she bring anything for herself?"

"A duffel. The rest will be shipped."

She reached for some of the cloth grocery bags, then said quickly, "I'm sorry for how I reacted when you told me Regina was coming. I know you must be thrilled."

He paused as he reached for a sack of kibble. "It's okay, Abby. You weren't hired to be a nanny, and frankly from what I've been hearing, that's not what she needs. I think those nannies got run off because Stella was ignoring her. For a kid, any attention is better than none."

Abby, too, paused and dared to look at him. His blue eyes seemed quiet, like deep pools. "That's sad," she said finally.

"I agree. Anyway, she needs me."

"Considering you came here to be a hermit, your life could get difficult."

"Not because of her. We stopped and signed her up for school. She starts tomorrow. She also understands my work habits. If she wants, she can spend time in the studio with me." He cocked a brow. "Unfortunately, now she's talking about getting a horse."

In spite of her lingering nerves, Abby laughed. "That's a job and a half."

"No kidding. I used to take care of them. Well, we'll see. I expect we'll jolt a while before we all settle in somehow."

He looked after his daughter and the running dog. "What I said about your job changing?"

She tensed again. "Yes?"

"I meant only that now there's somebody who has to get regular meals." Then he flashed a grin at her. "And I don't mean the dog. General is her job."

"His name is General?"

"Rally for short. And no, don't ask me to explain. It just is."

Abby helped with the groceries, then began stowing them as Rory took the rest of the dog food out to the barn. One forty-pound bag had taken up residence on the floor of the spacious pantry, however. Along with two stainless steel bowls on a stand.

Shrugging, Abby put the stand in one corner of the kitchen with a rug under it and filled one of the bowls with water. That dog must need a good drink by now.

She heard the girl and dog burst in through the front door before Rory had finished putting the dog food away. Apparently General, or Rally, knew exactly what he needed and where it was. The clacking of claws on wood alerted her, and Abby backed away to a safe distance. Moments later, the Great Dane skidded through the door and found the water bowl. He was not a neat drinker.

Regina followed more hesitantly. "Hi," the girl said. She looked so much like her father but with a heart-shaped face.

"Hi," Abby answered. "I'm Abby."

"I figured. Lots of people call me Gina, but I like Regina better."

"Regina it is."

A shy smile. "Rally's a good dog. You don't need to be afraid of him."

"He looks as big as a horse."

"I'm sorry he's so messy."

"It's just water."

Regina gave a little laugh. "He drools, too. Lots of big dogs do. But it's my job to clean up after him."

"Is he allowed on furniture?"

Regina nodded. "He likes to take up a whole couch. I hope Dad has two."

"Dad has plenty," Abby answered wryly, thinking of the huge living room with its equally huge furniture, including two oversized sofas and full-sized piano. White carpeting. She wondered how often she'd be spot-treating it.

Just then Rory came in the back door and joined them.

Rally drained the bowl and looked around.

"Does he need more water?" Abby asked. "I can get it."

But Rally seemed to have another interest. He walked slowly over to Abby, who tried not to shrink. Heavens, she was almost eye-to-eye with him.

"Rally, sit," Regina said mildly.

The dog obeyed, but Abby had to laugh because even as he sat in front of her, his tail was wagging like mad. "He does seem friendly."

"Hold your hand palm up and let him sniff you," Regina said. "Then you can pet him and you'll be friends for life."

Friends for life sounded like the best alternative with an animal so big. She glanced at Rory and found him watching with amusement.

Still unsure but determined not to show it, Abby held her hand out as directed. Rally leaned his head forward and sniffed at her hand. His breath was powerful, matching his size, she guessed.

"Now you can scratch him behind the ear," Regina said.

Abby did so and enjoyed the way the dog suddenly grinned and wagged his tail even harder.

"Friends for life," Rory said. "But seriously, Abby, Regina cleans up after him and feeds him."

"Right," Regina said. "Can I see my room now? And you said you have a big studio. Am I allowed in there?"

"Any time you want."

The two of them headed upstairs to pick the girl's room, but Rally remained behind. Abby stood looking back at him, wondering if he wanted more petting, more water, or just to hold her prisoner. She had no idea.

Drool started to drip from his jaw. He extended a big tongue to slurp it away. And for some reason that made him look less dangerous to her. Big, sappy dog, she thought.

She extended her hand again, and this time he leaned into it, encouraging her scratches. Okay then. Not a prisoner.

Almost laughing at herself, she moved. He backed away, watching with his head cocked. After she refilled his water bowl, he drank half of it. Apparently satisfied now, he amazed her by loping for the stairs, following Regina's voice.

This could work, Abby thought. Well, it kind of had to. And thank goodness this was such a big house. The dog had made this huge kitchen feel small. Briefly.

Regina seemed nice enough, a great relief since she'd been expecting a hellion. Of course, that could change, but right now everything appeared to be all right.

She caught herself as she started pulling out the ingredients for dinner. She had developed a terrible habit of expecting everything to turn out badly. Everything. She didn't even know that child, but here she was making assumptions that it would all go to hell.

"Thank you, Porter," she muttered to her absent ex-husband as she began to slice thawed chicken breasts into small cubes for chicken Alfredo. She needed a major attitude adjustment of some kind. She just wasn't sure how to do it.

For what seemed like ages she'd been living in a sea of pain and betrayal, and it wasn't as if she could wash it away with a shower. Trust had been shattered, suspicion had become a way of life and apparently so had the belief that everything would go south eventually.

Not a very optimistic outlook for a twenty-six-year-old woman. She had a lot of years left, and unless she wanted to become a paranoid recluse, she needed to get over this hump.

Hump? Right now it looked bigger than the Rocky Mountains she could see out back.

For over a week, everything went well enough. Regina came home from school, grabbed a snack and either disappeared to her bedroom or out to the barn to do her schoolwork. She pretty much left Abby alone. While Regina was at school, Rally hung out with Rory, whether he was in the barn or walking the fields. Abby grew sick of cleaning the same bathrooms and bedrooms and doing the laundry and keeping up with the dust.

Dust ended up everywhere, not surprising given

that autumn had dried out the area and quickened the breeze, but on so many polished surfaces, from kitchen to floors to railings, it was a nuisance to keep up with and couldn't be ignored.

She served Rory and Regina their dinner in the dining room, and ate her own in the kitchen before she cleaned up the dishes. Usually Rory showed for dinner, and she could hear him and Regina chatting and laughing. A couple of times he didn't return from the barn, leaving his daughter to eat alone. She didn't seem to mind.

For the first time it struck Abby that this job could bore her to madness. She needed something to do for herself, a project or a hobby. She'd always had a job, but nothing like this one that made so few real demands on her.

Every room had a TV tucked somewhere, including her own, and a satellite dish outside provided a wide selection of viewing, but TV couldn't occupy her for long.

She was used to being much busier. Except for cooking, this job could have been handled in two or three days a week.

Well, Rory had told her she was free to do as she liked, so she could go to town and visit friends who would probably only try to sympathize with her about Porter and Joan, or question her about the habits of her famous boss. Neither appealed to her.

Standing in the middle of the stainless-steel kitchen that desperately needed *something* to bring it to life, she looked out the wide window over the sink. In the distance she could see trees tossing in a freshening wind and tumbleweeds rolling like gigantic bowling balls. Toward the mountains, she saw heavy, dark clouds building.

A change in the weather would be nice. *Any* change would be nice. "Gah!" she said aloud.

Regina should be the one bored to death, she thought, but the girl seemed quite happy. Also willing to ignore Abby. She thought about Regina's room, and while it was beautifully decorated, it was rather Spartan in an emotional sense. It lacked personal belongings, other than a few things she had brought with her. Was that how she had lived with her mother?

If so, she felt sorry for the girl. She wondered if she should offer to take her to town to get some decorations to make the room her own. But maybe that would be overstepping.

It was almost a relief to hear the front door open, even if it meant only that Regina would race to the pantry, grab a snack and a can of soda from the fridge and vanish again. Movement. She needed movement. Life. Activity. More than dust and bathrooms, laundry and cooking.

Regina popped in as always, with a shy, "Hi," then headed for the fridge.

Abby broke the routine. "How was your day?"

Regina paused, can of soda in hand, and turned to look at her. The refrigerator door swung shut behind her. Then she smiled, that same heart-melting smile her father sometimes displayed.

"What's up?" she asked Abby.

Now how was she supposed to answer that? Finally Abby grabbed what little courage she had left and spoke the truth. "I am bored with cleaning, cooking and washing. There's not enough to do. So I asked how your day was."

Regina tilted her head to one side, then a giggle burst out of her. "Dad said I wasn't to bother you."

"Oh, please bother me."

Regina's giggle turned into a laugh. "Okay." She pulled out a chair at the table and sat. "My day was great. I'm making some friends, although I think might be because of who my dad is."

The statement shocked Abby. That a girl this age should even have to wonder about such things? It wasn't right. "Or maybe they just like you."

"I don't know. That's the problem with having famous parents. You can't be sure."

Abby stepped closer, sympathy rising in her. After her own experience, she completely connected with what Regina was saying. Lack of trust had entered her own life, too. "I never thought of that."

"I have to. I've watched people suck up to my parents because of who they were, and not all of them are nice. So you have to be careful, that's all."

"That's sad."

Regina popped the top on her soda. "It's worse for my dad, I think. He can do stuff for people. I can't do anything for anyone. Do you want one of my Cokes? I mean pop. That's what everyone calls it here, I guess."

"Thanks. I have coffee." Abby grabbed a mug and came to sit cautiously at the table. "I didn't mean to hold you up. I know you have homework and stuff."

"Rally's maybe wondering where I am, but there's not a whole lot of homework. So you're bored? I wondered."

Abby tried to smile, feeling like a bit of a fool for

even mentioning it to the girl. It wasn't *her* problem. "Was it that obvious?"

"Well, I haven't talked to you much, but cleaning all the time would get pretty boring for *me*." She furrowed her brow. "No hobbies?"

"Not yet. I used to be busy all the time. This is new for me."

"I guess it's new for both of us. When I lived with Mom, she had me signed up for everything. I like being able to choose what to do with my time." Again that head tilt. Abby wondered if she'd learned it from Rally. "That could change, I guess. Do you like to do stuff on computers?"

Abby thought about it. "You mean like go online? I was never much into that, although maybe I should poke around. I might even learn something."

Regina giggled again. "Well, Dad's got plenty of computers. Maybe you should look around and see if there's something you like. You can even take classes online if you're desperate enough."

"Really?"

"Really." Regina rolled her eyes. "Where have you been hiding?"

"In a marriage and a job. And with friends. Like I said, busy all the time."

Regina grinned. "Maybe I should stop straightening up my room."

"Don't you dare. More cleaning is not the answer." But Abby had to laugh. She was really liking this child.

"I can't wait until my stuff gets here," Regina remarked.

"Your stuff?"

"Yeah, Mom's supposed to send all my clothes and other things. There was a limit to what I could get on Dad's plane, especially once I said I was bringing my dog."

"He *would* take up a lot of room."

"And weight. So yeah, I only brought a few things with me."

Abby hesitated, feeling her heart go out to the child. "Are you glad you came? Or are you homesick?"

"Oh, I'm glad. I never saw my mom anyway, and I hated those nannies. I had to be perfect all the time, and a lot of them didn't like General. If you don't like my dog, you don't like me."

An interesting perspective, Abby thought. She could appreciate it, though. "Rally's a good dog."

"Yup." Regina stood up. "I need to get out to the barn before Dad looks up and notices the time. Or before Rally starts driving him nuts cuz he knows I ought to be there now. Heck, Rally probably heard the school bus even inside the barn. He's good at that. Grab yourself one of the laptop computers. I'm sure Dad won't mind, and they're all hooked up to the internet."

She grabbed a small bag of chips, said a cheery goodbye and headed out back toward the barn. Not five minutes later Abby saw girl and dog racing around outside with the sheer joy of being alive and together.

Maybe she should have been born a dog. Nothing she could do about that now, so she went to get a laptop from the front room. Looking around the web might lead her to something interesting.

An hour later, she set the table for dinner. Two places

in the dining room, her solitary one in the kitchen. Spaghetti and meatballs, homemade sauce. Crusty garlic bread and a tossed salad. She wondered how many would eat.

Before she could fill serving dishes, however, she heard the back door open. A minute later, Regina entered the kitchen carrying two plates that she put on the kitchen table.

"What?" Abby asked.

"This is silly" was all the girl said. In another minute, she had three places set at the kitchen table.

"But your dad…"

"Doesn't mind," said the deep familiar voice of Rory. He stood in the kitchen doorway, smiling. "Do you?"

"Of course not."

"Good, because I was starting to feel like a feudal lord in that dining room. All I need to fill it are about twenty minions. Tonight you sit. Regina and I will wait on you."

Abby felt her cheeks heat. "That's not…"

"It's perfectly right," he said. "Now sit down, Abby. Regina is looking forward to this."

Abby looked at Regina, who was beaming. "I am. I never got to do this at Mom's. You might have to give me instructions."

"I can do the instructions," Rory said. "I wasn't always a too-big-for-my-own-hat superstar, you know. I grew up on a ranch and everyone pitched in. I even used to cook and wash dishes."

Regina giggled. "You do dishes?"

Rory pretended to scowl at her. "I do indeed."

"This I want to see," his daughter answered pertly.

Deciding she really had no choice in the matter,

and honestly not minding it because it was fun to watch, Abby sat at the table while Rory and Regina worked to serve the meal. Rory gave gentle instructions, but only when needed, allowing his daughter to do most of the task. Abby's help was needed only when they didn't know where to look for something, such as the ladle.

"Really sorry, that's me," muttered Rory. "I ought to know what's in my own kitchen."

Regina answered. "Your head's too busy filling that hat."

He laughed. But then Regina turned and gave him a big hug around his waist. "You're cool, Dad. And the important thing is writing your songs. I like that new one you're working on." Then she went back to serving dinner.

"It's giving me fits," he admitted. "Long ago, before I made it, I used to have more melodies and lyrics floating around in my head than I could use. Feels like the well went dry."

Which, thought Abby, was probably what he'd meant about this place rebuilding him. He'd lost something essential, and he wanted it back. She knew the feeling all too well, except in her case she'd finally reached the point where she didn't want any of it back. But for him it had to be different. This was not the kind of divorce any artist wanted, she was sure. Watching him move around the kitchen, he didn't appear troubled, but he sure appeared attractive. The background sizzle he always elicited in her had arisen again. Attracted to her boss? Not good.

Soon they were gathered in a cozy group around the kitchen table. Abby complimented the food generously and Regina said, "I'd like to learn how to make the spaghetti sauce by myself. I could have my friends over for a spaghetti party."

That caused Rory to lift his head. "So you're making friends?"

"Of course. It's easy when your daddy is Rory McLane."

Abby tensed, watching Rory's reaction to that. Sadness seemed to flicker over his face. "Sorry, kiddo."

Regina shrugged. "They'll get over it soon enough. Then I'll find out who's for real."

One corner of his mouth lifted. "How old are you again?"

She giggled. "Old enough. It's okay, Dad. And actually, I like it. Here I'm meeting kids who don't have famous parents. It's different."

His smile faded again. He looked as if he wanted to say something, then decided against it. Regina didn't miss the cues, though.

"I know," she said. "Mom was into the whole scene. Who I could hang out with, all that. I almost never got to meet ordinary kids." She twirled her fork in her spaghetti. "How can I ever be ordinary if I'm always in a box?"

"A box?" Rory asked.

"A box. That's how I felt." But she didn't seem to have any other way to describe it.

Abby listened to this, both troubled and amazed. She had never before considered what it might be like to be Regina, to have two famous parents. She wished she could ask questions, but Regina had moved on to talking about other things, like getting a horse, leaving Rory to look vaguely troubled.

* * *

After dinner, having been dismissed from dish duty, Abby followed her usual custom of disappearing into her suite at the back of the house. It was a cozy space, decorated pleasantly in warm yellows and blues, clearly designed with a woman in mind by the decorator.

She had a bedroom, a sitting area with a small kitchenette and her own bathroom with a separate shower and a walk-in whirlpool tub. Elegance beyond any she had ever known. All by itself it was a livable apartment, and from the windows in the sitting area she had a beautiful view of the mountains and the barn where Rory was working. She even had her own private entry from outside.

Nicer than any dwelling in her entire life, and even though she enjoyed it, sometimes she felt a bit like an impostor. She didn't come from wealth and saw herself as an outsider looking in. She wondered if Rory ever felt that way.

Her parents had owned a small catalog store that had thrived for many years, but had eventually gone broke with the upsurge of internet shopping. Abby had started college a few years late as she tried to help them through the hump, but finally her dad had found a job in Colorado Springs and they had moved away. They'd sent small sums to help with her school expenses, then she'd met and eventually married Porter. When she'd had come back here as a new bride, she'd been hired by Joan to look after Joan's dress boutique, a small business with a select and limited clientele. Everything had seemed perfect.

Until Porter announced he was leaving with Joan.

She supposed, in those moments when she was able to find some gratitude, that she was lucky they'd decided to leave town. Joan sold her boutique, Porter found a job as a clerk with a big law firm in Idaho and the two had vanished...after Porter sold his family house in town.

Since his betrayal, she'd been working as a waitress at the truck stop, nursing her wounds, unable to see the possibility of ever getting herself unstuck, emotionally or physically. She'd had to rent a small apartment, all she could afford, and the community college offered no classes beyond the ones she'd already completed. She'd been looking at a bleak future until she saw the ad for this job.

Now she could sock away enough money to go to the state university. If she could hang on long enough.

She wished she hadn't told Regina how bored she was. She ought to be feeling awfully grateful, boredom aside. Life had given her a stepping stone to a brighter future, even if she no longer knew what she wanted that future to hold.

Sitting with Regina and Rory at dinner tonight had awakened some old dreams. Or maybe they'd been illusions. Illusions of long years with Porter, of children of their own, of happy family gatherings. Of having a family again. Her parents were now so far away she could only afford to drive down to see them once in a great while, and her dad had a heart condition that prevented him from attempting the trip.

So here she sat, stuck in Conard County, with a whole bunch of unhappy memories. All of it her own fault, she supposed.

It had been sweet of Regina to include her in dinner

tonight, but she couldn't expect that to continue. She was an employee, and her employer had been frank about coming here for solitude.

Given that, though, it was kind of surprising how happy he'd been about getting his daughter. She'd have loved to know the story behind that.

She stared at the stack of library books beside her bed, but didn't feel much like reading. She remembered the computer out in the living room, and in a moment of genuine curiosity about her rooms, she started investigating spaces she hadn't yet really looked at.

Oh, she'd put away her clothes in the dresser and surveyed the kitchen appliances and utensils, but she hadn't examined the desk in one corner of her sitting room. It looked like a simple writing desk with one bank of drawers up the side, but she hadn't needed a desk yet.

Rising, she went over and began to open drawers. The top one, which appeared merely to be a decorative front and had resisted her efforts to pull it open, turned out to have a tip-down front. When she did that, it slid out and revealed yet another laptop. Regina hadn't been kidding about them being all over the house, like the TVs.

This one was hardwired into a wall connection, but the cord was long enough that she was able to pull it out and set it on top of the desk. The drawer then closed most of the way and she pulled the secretarial chair back in front of it.

This could be cool, she thought. Maybe she'd research those online courses Regina had mentioned, in case she had enough money to take one before long.

Maybe she could get a head start on going back for her degree.

Her heart leaped a little at the prospect.

She should have checked this out sooner. But ever since coming here, housekeeper or not, she had felt a little like an interloper and had tried to respect privacy. She didn't open drawers outside the kitchen. She didn't poke into closets. Sooner or later she supposed she'd have to or the closets would get dusty. She needed to ask Rory what her limits were.

Just as she was about to turn the laptop on, she heard a quiet knock at her door. It was so unusual that she started. Immediately she wondered if Regina needed help.

Jumping up, she went to answer it and found Rory standing there, the fingers of one hand tucked into his jeans pocket. He stood back a foot in the short hallway, as if to give her space.

"Sorry to intrude," he said, smiling, "but I wondered if you could give me a few minutes. Out in the living room."

"Sure," she answered promptly, oddly relieved that he didn't want to come in here, although she didn't know why. Too intimate? That was silly. He owned the place.

Then she got nervous. Had she done something wrong? Was he going to fire her? Other than her one ugly, incautious remark, she couldn't imagine that she'd done anything terrible.

Of course, not having done anything wrong didn't mean much, as she had already learned the hard way.

"Want some coffee?" he asked as they passed the kitchen.

"No, thank you."

"Grab a seat. I'll be right with you."

She perched on the edge of one of the heavy, large armchairs. Built solidly of wood with blue cushions, their massiveness helped counter the immense size of the room, as did the two huge couches and the piano in one corner. You could probably play basketball in here, she thought, trying to keep a sense of amusement. She was failing miserably.

He wasn't long, returning with a mug of coffee. He looked around. "You know, this isn't exactly a cozy room, is it? We could shout from opposite ends of it."

Her tension began to ease, and a small laugh escaped her. "Good for entertaining."

"I didn't come here to entertain, although I suppose it could happen. This is what happens when you hand a contractor and a decorator a few ideas and cut them loose." He shook his head. "Kitchen?"

"Please." Maybe there she wouldn't feel so tiny and insignificant.

They adjourned to the kitchen table and sat facing each other across it.

"This feels almost human-sized," he remarked. He leaned back in his chair and regarded her over the top of his mug as he took a sip. She felt the attraction again, the way something about him seemed to draw her. It wasn't just that he was good-looking, although he was, but some other aura that made her feel the stirrings of passion that she had tried to cut out of her life. No wonder Rory McLane was a superstar. Every woman probably felt the same way about him.

She dared to ask, "Did you really just cut them loose?"

"The builder and decorator? Yeah. See, that's been part of the problem. I've been so busy all the time with everything I've *had* to do that I haven't been writing any decent music of my own, or running any other part of my life. So this is where I get to. A hermitage that could double as a small hotel." He shook his head a little. "I shouldn't complain. I've been damn lucky."

"Talented, too," she suggested.

"Well, lately I've been wondering about that. But that's not what I wanted to talk with you about."

Anxiety returned, creeping along her nerve endings. "Did I do something wrong?"

"No!" He appeared startled. "Nothing like that. I just thought it might help you to understand some of what's happening here. Yes, I know the ground rules I originally set out. You pretty much go your way and I go mine. But now there's Regina, and a dog, and things got a little more complicated for everyone. The way things are going, there's probably even going to be a horse or two, some slumber parties, some other parties...." He paused, looking momentarily overwhelmed, then continued. "So I thought you might be more comfortable if you knew some things, rather than spending your time wondering what the heck happened."

As her anxiety eased, she was able to smile. "You make it sound like an invasion."

"It probably will be, by the time all's said and done." His smile was a little crooked. "Just another way for Stella to get even."

"Stella?"

"My ex. Regina's mother. Do you keep up with country music?"

She shook her head, feeling inexplicably embarrassed. "No, sorry."

"No apology needed. Suffice it to say, my ex is a big deal in her own right, only she eats it all up. The only person she saw more than me and her band during our marriage was her hairdresser and her plastic surgeon."

Abby couldn't help it. She clapped her hand over her mouth to stifle her laugh.

"Exactly," he said. "I probably shouldn't sound so critical. Me, I can age gracefully. She's a woman, and youth and beauty are part of her trade. Sorry comment on society, but that's the way it is. Anyway, when we split, there was a custody fight and I lost. The judge was sympathetic to the idea that a girl needed her mama more than her dad. I figured I had to wait until Regina was old enough to decide who she wanted to live with, and put up with our long separations."

"But something happened."

One corner of his mouth lifted. "You could say Regina happened. She created more trouble for Stella than a pack of weasels let loose in the house."

This time Abby let the laugh escape. "She doesn't strike me that way."

"Me, neither. Oh, I'm not gonna claim she's perfect. What kid is? But the constant loss of nannies finally became enough to make Stella forget how mad she was at me." He shifted, looking down. "I often think the only reason she wanted full custody to begin with was because it was another way to get back at me. Guess I was right. So Stella gave me full custody and I have my daughter back."

Everything inside Abby softened. "I could tell how happy that made you. I'm glad."

"Me, too. She's out of that plastic, over-regimented environment. Stella is all about appearances, and I was afraid she'd make Regina that way, too. Hasn't happened yet, evidently."

Abby decided not to address that. After all, today was the first time she'd really spent any time with Regina. She liked the girl, but she didn't really know her yet.

"Anyway," he said, "that brings us to the invasion. I'm sorry if it put you out."

"It hasn't put me out at all," Abby said swiftly. She almost squirmed as she remembered her initial reaction and how that must have felt to him. "I'm sorry I blurted that out about not being hired for childcare."

"Well, it's true, you weren't. Don't worry about it. And I'm not asking you to step up to that plate now. That's not why we're talking. I just want you to know the background, because it must have felt like a whirlwind hit."

"It was a surprise, but not that momentous. I like Regina."

"If she bugs you too much, let me know." He leaned forward and put his cup down. "I'm not the world's best dad. I get lost inside my own head sometimes. Well, I'm trying to. Been a while since I had time to do that. But I'm going to ask you something."

She waited, trying to look anywhere but right at him. She was afraid he would read her reaction to him all over her face. Appalling to realize she wanted him. A man who could have any woman in the world. A man who saw her as nothing but a housekeeper. Did she have a nose for trouble, or what?

"If she lets you know in any way that she feels I'm neglecting her because I get too absorbed in my composing, will you tell me?"

Abby nodded. "Okay, I can do that."

"Thanks."

She thought that would end their conversation, but instead he rose, refilled his mug and returned to the table.

"So what's your story, Abby?" he asked, his tone surprisingly kind.

It was that kindness that got to her. It felt like a long time since anyone had expressed a truly kind interest in her. Her friends had grown angry on her behalf, and too many people had been trying to avoid looking at her, as if she made them uneasy. His frankness, the gentleness of his tone...well, they made her throat and chest tighten.

Oh, man, she didn't want to start weeping. She tried to draw some steadying breaths, and finally managed to say, "Old familiar story. Husband runs off with another woman. Who happened to be my boss until then. Nothing unusual in that, I guess."

"Maybe not, but that doesn't make it any easier. I'm sorry."

She couldn't answer. She became fascinated by the pattern on the tabletop. Easier than looking at him and perhaps seeing pity.

He astonished her by reaching across the table and lightly covering her hand with his. "We all have some healing to do," he said quietly. "Maybe this place will help us find some peace. Good night, Abby. Thanks for listening."

She didn't move until she heard him reach the top of the stairs. Then she stood and turned off the coffeepot, rinsing it out so that it would be ready for morning.

As she turned out the kitchen light and walked back to her rooms, she wondered what to make of what had just happened. The guy had reached out to her, shared some of his problems, asked about hers. Then he'd gotten up and walked away.

Had she repulsed him somehow? She wouldn't be surprised considering the way Porter had bailed on her. Something about her had to be very wrong. She just couldn't figure out what it was.

Much to her amazement, before she could close her suite door behind her, Rally trotted in. Still afraid to get into a disagreement with an animal so big, she readied for bed, leaving the door open, and finally climbed beneath crisp sheets and a puffy comforter.

The dog leaped up beside her and put his big head next to hers and his paw across her waist.

A hug from a dog. This might be her absolute nadir, but she didn't care. He comforted her.

And maybe that was what she really needed.

Chapter Three

The clouds that had lumbered over the mountains moved through without dropping any rain or snow, but they left a deep chill in their wake. Frost covered the ground in the early morning hours and Regina started bundling up before heading out to catch the school bus.

Rory had returned to spending his days in his barn studio, and Abby spent her free time online, looking for classes she might be able to afford that would give her transferable credits for when she returned to school.

A kind of anticipatory excitement began to fill her, and all her gloominess and boredom blew away. So many subjects interested her, and she enjoyed looking into the requirements for a number of majors, trying to decide what might suit her best. It was a step toward a future, the first real one she'd taken since Porter's betrayal.

Her improved outlook brightened everything around her, and when she looked up from her computer to realize that Regina was already returning from school one afternoon, she was astonished at how the time had flown. She hadn't even started dinner, and her mind immediately shifted gears as she glanced at the clock and tried to decide what she could manage quickly.

Regina had taken to popping in to say hi when she got home, spending only a few minutes in the kitchen with Abby. Today was no different. She grabbed her can of soda and a bag of pretzels and sat down at the table, indicating the laptop.

"Getting anywhere?"

"Your suggestion about looking for online classes was great."

Regina screwed up her face. "I can hardly wait to be done with school."

Abby felt immediate concern. "Something bad happen?"

Regina shook her head. "Just boring. I'd rather be riding a horse."

Abby laughed. "I keep hearing that."

"Dad isn't listening so well." Regina flashed a grin and shrugged. "He will eventually. Every girl should have a horse."

"I'm sure most girls your age would agree."

"Did you have one?"

Abby shook her head. She'd had a period of infatuation with horses, a lot of girls did, but she'd lived in town and her parents couldn't afford it. They'd taken her out for a few trail rides at the Ironheart ranch, but that had been it. "Not possible." Then she shifted the subject purposefully. She didn't want Regina to try to drag her into the middle of her campaign for a horse. That was solely between her and Rory. "I need to come up with a quick dinner. I lost track of time."

"I won't die if we eat late," Regina said, grabbing another pretzel. "Who knows if Dad will even surface?"

He'd been doing a good job of it most of the time. Given what Rory had said when he'd first arrived, Abby was surprised by how often he turned up for dinner. Of course, since Regina joined him in the studio most days after school, he probably found it hard to forget time.

She wondered if that was giving him any problem with his composing. She hoped not.

Regina picked up her bag of pretzels. "I'd better get out there. Rally is probably getting frantic."

Just then, as if in answer to her thoughts, Rally's feet could be heart clacking and padding down the hall from the back door. He zoomed into the kitchen and began to lick Regina's cheek. She shrieked a giggle.

"Somebody was missing you, girl," Rory called from the hall, sounding amused.

"Sorry, Dad, I was talking with Abby."

Abby felt pleasant anticipation humming along her nerves. She always enjoyed seeing Rory, however rarely or briefly, and she was growing more impressed with how ordinary he seemed. Fame and wealth hadn't gone to his head as far as she could tell. But more than that, he filled out jeans and a Western shirt better than any man she'd ever seen. Broad shoulders, narrow hips, just the sight of him seemed to zoom straight to her core.

But that was the only way he was ordinary. She felt almost guilty the way everything inside her seemed to leap at the sight of him. Guilty and maybe a little silly, like a fan with a crush. She'd even sneaked online to listen to a couple of his songs, to learn something about the music that was so important to him. Listening, she had wondered how she'd managed to miss this phenom for so long.

But it was her guilty secret and pleasure. She didn't want to lose her job because she acted like a starstruck fool around him, nor did she want to cause the kinds of problems Regina had mentioned. She *did* wonder, however, if he felt as used as Regina had sensed. That would be awful.

She ought to know. She felt she had been used by Porter and Joan. How long must they have been carrying on behind her back? Using her for cover to prevent talk? She had no idea, and she wasn't sure she wanted to know.

Bad enough that she felt branded by shame. She wasn't going to make it worse be allowing herself to go overboard about Rory. She was just a housekeeper. She needed to remember that.

But Rory didn't come into the kitchen. She heard music coming from the piano in the living room and perked up, listening. It was a gentle melody, almost mournful, yet achingly beautiful.

Regina fell silent, listening, too. Then she hopped up and went to the living room.

Abby didn't feel she had the right to follow, but the

melody, soon accompanied by some minor chords, held her riveted.

A weight fell on Abby's thigh and she looked down to see that Rally had laid his head there. Not since that one night had he come into her room, but now he looked up with those sad eyes, as if asking for something.

She scratched his huge head. His tail wagged, but only a little. Was he hungry? Regina always fed him at dinnertime and it was still too early. Maybe a treat?

The melody still drifted from the living room, but the dog's intervention broke the spell and she rose. There were treats in the pantry, and no one had told her she couldn't give one to the dog. A soft bacon chew settled him down, then she leaned against the doorway listening to the music.

She could hear the stops and restarts as Rory seemed to be searching for something just right. She heard no voices, just the music. It would have been nice to keep on listening, but inevitably she remembered she had a job and needed to figure out a fast dinner.

Sighing, she began to hunt in the refrigerator and pantry when she would have vastly preferred to creep into the living room and just sit and listen.

Magic was being created out there, and she wished she could be part of it.

Dinner was a tossed-together affair. Rory didn't return to his studio, but instead staked out the living room and piano. Eventually Regina popped into the kitchen to say good-night. That was Abby's cue to head for her apartment.

But just as she was turning out the light, Rory's

voice startled her from across the foyer. "What do you think?"

She paused, her hand on the switch. "The music?"

He smiled faintly. "The almost music, yes."

"It's beautiful. I love it."

"It's mournful." He paused. "Sometimes I guess you need to mourn. Unless you're busy, come and sit with me. I'd like your reactions."

Her reactions? She knew nothing about music at all. But the desire to be with him overrode every other consideration. "Coffee?" she asked.

"Yeah, I'll probably be up most of the night. Thanks."

So she brewed another pot and ten minutes later carried two hot mugs into the living room. He was sitting at the piano, staring into space, noodling some keys. She wondered where to put his coffee, but he pointed to a nearby end table without saying anything. Then she sat in one of those huge chairs with hers.

He continued to stare at nothing, probably more involved with what was going on inside him as he touched occasional keys as if trying them out. He seemed lost in another world, and she wondered why he needed her at all.

She rested her coffee on the end table, then closed her eyes and let her head fall back. Interrupted though the music was, often changing to random notes as if he were seeking something, she found it easy to let it carry her away. A while later he spoke.

"Abby?"

She opened her eyes without moving her head. "Yes?"

"Were you sleeping?"

"No, I was listening." She turned her head just

enough to see him, thinking how gorgeous he was. She hadn't met many men who looked like a feast for the eyes. This one did.

"What do you think? Is it like a dirge?"

That popped her head up. "Not at all. It's melancholy, but a beautiful melancholy. It's kind of like…" She hesitated. "I shouldn't say anything. I don't know music."

"Most of the people I play and sing for don't know music. They know what they like is all. I'm not asking a technical question. I want to know how it makes you feel."

She rolled her head a little more. "Play the melody part again. With the chords."

So he did, letting the notes ripple through the room. It stopped too soon.

"So?" he asked.

"It makes me feel like I'm drifting on a warm, slow river all by myself. It's pretty, but kind of lonely." Making those statements seemed awfully bold, but they were as true an expression as she could find.

He nodded. "It's not my usual," he admitted. "But it's my heart."

Touched, she felt an unexpected sadness for him. So he felt lonesome, too? But then she wondered if everyone didn't at times. As if something was lacking or missing. She gathered her courage. "It's like looking for something you can't quite remember."

His smile grew. "That's it. That's what I was trying for."

"Then you succeeded because I think it's going to follow me into my dreams. It's…haunting."

"It'll drive my manager and agent crazy." He sighed

and turned back to the keyboard, running through it again, his fingers delicate on the keys. A rippling current of music and magic ran through the room.

"There's a part of me," he said as he played, "that vanished a long time ago. That's what I came back here to find." As he spoke, his baritone began to echo the music. Not lyrics, not yet, but she guessed they were starting to come to him.

He stopped playing and held out an arm toward her. "Come sit over here with me," he said. "I think we're both a little mournful and wistful."

Nervously, but feeling a kind of hope anyway, she rose and walked over. He drew her down on the bench beside him until their shoulders were touching.

"Lost long ago. Homesickness for something we can't quite remember. Dreams?"

She wasn't sure how to answer. He began playing again, and she watched his hands glide over the keys. This time he played the haunting melody more strongly, and this time he didn't pause as missing notes seemed to spring from his fingertips. When he finished, the last notes trailed slowly away.

Then he smiled at her, causing her heart to leap. "You're a great Muse," he said. "And I've stolen your evening. Sorry."

"You just gave me a wonderful gift. I loved it." The words came straight from her heart. She felt blessed to have shared this with him, to have entered however briefly into his creative process and to have been one of the first to hear a truly incredible piece of music.

Much as she didn't want to, she rose to go to her rooms. She sensed he wanted to be alone now. The haunting notes of the melody followed her all the way down the hall to her quarters. She was reluctant to leave them behind, but since she'd taken to leaving her door open a few inches since Regina's arrival, she didn't entirely close out the music.

Changes had begun to happen inside her, she realized. They frightened her a bit. Little by little she was exposing her heart again, to a man and his daughter.

She ought to know better after Porter. She thought she *had* known better, but apparently not. Somehow she had to quell her growing desire for him.

If there was one thing she was sure about, it was that there could be no future with Rory McLane, so why have a messy present?

Rory was sorry to see her go, but he knew he'd intruded on her evening. He'd never meant for her to be at his beck and call round the clock, and considered her evening hours to be sacrosanct. Yet tonight he'd intruded.

It wasn't just the music, although that had been part of it. He occasionally liked some feedback from a naive listener, and from what she'd said, he gathered Abby didn't know much about who he was or his music.

That was fine by him. Running back to Conard County he had hoped to escape a lot of that. Oh, he had friends in the business, people who shared all the highs and lows, the stresses, the good times and bad. But it was like a closed loop, and one day he'd realized that it had closed him in and cut off part of him.

Maybe it was ridiculous of him to want to reach back in time to a boy he'd once been. After all, life happened to everyone, changed everyone, and twenty years had happened to him, for better or worse.

But that feeling of being homesick for something you couldn't quite remember—that was a powerful feeling. Abby had nailed that one. It had been troubling him more and more until he had decided that he needed to get away for a while.

But even here in his hidey-hole, life wasn't what it had been when he was sharing a ranch with his parents as a kid. No, he was surrounded by luxury, living a self-indulgent life. How many people had the choice of throwing over their work for months to take a sabbatical? Not many.

He was a lucky man and he knew it. Luckier now that he had custody of Regina. Lucky that for the first time since the divorce he'd have her for both upcoming holidays.

At least Abby hadn't seemed to mind being called upon to be his audience for a while. He wondered if the song was going to be about her, because he sensed in her many of the same discontents and sorrows he knew. Undoubtedly a different degree, undoubtedly not exactly the same, but still he felt an emotional recognition of something in her.

The little bit she'd said about her marriage made him wonder about her. Deserted by her husband for her former boss? Ugly. Wounding. He couldn't imagine the skein of bad feelings that must have left her with. At least with Stella, he hadn't been either surprised or especially wounded when she decided to move on. Except for Regina it would have been a clean, cheerful split.

He frowned a little as he thought about Stella,

though. She'd used him like a ladder, and he'd been a young fool, full of himself and his success, when she'd leaped aboard. Through him she'd managed to get enough exposure to leapfrog over some of the dues most folks had to pay.

But that was okay, too. Lots of people did that. Well, okay except for Regina. Stella had used the girl as she used everything else in life, and for that Rory felt a deep, unforgiving anger.

He realized angry notes were coming out of the piano now. Well, there was another song on the way, he guessed. But he didn't want to wake everyone up, so he closed the keyboard, grabbed his mug and went to get some fresh coffee. Maybe it was time to head out to the studio again, where he could bang away all he wanted. If he could turn anger into sarcasm, he might have another winner on his hands.

But winning was no longer his primary goal. He needed a deeper satisfaction, and that need had grown with the years, rather than diminishing.

Coffee in hand, he paused in the T-shaped hallway. In one direction lay Abby's rooms. In the other the back door.

The more he was around that woman, the more he wanted her. Nothing about her was plastic, as far as he could see. A wounded soul, but a genuine one. So maybe he should be kind to her and keep his heated thoughts to himself. She didn't need any more wounding. Come to think of it, neither did he.

He noted that her door was open a few inches, although he could see no light inside. Whether she wanted to or not, she had begun in small ways to look after Regina, and he suspected leaving her door open like that was an invitation to his daughter should she need something during the night. Also a signal that he needn't worry about the girl if he went out to the barn at night.

A kindly heart. He hoped he wasn't imagining it. Life had taught him to be distrustful of people's motives. They often wanted something from him. Most of the time he didn't mind. If it was within his power, he liked to help. What he didn't like was feeling that he'd been used. He'd much rather a man come up to him and flat-out ask him for an audition at a studio than have someone fawn all over him, pretending to be a friend when it truth he wanted Rory to take his audition tape to his manager.

It wasn't always possible to tell when friendships were real until some stress revealed that reality behind the false smiles. Like Stella. He'd honestly thought that woman had loved him. If she ever had, it was so long ago that he'd no longer be willing to testify to it.

And of course he had groupies throwing themselves at him all the time. Women interested in Rory McLane the star, not Rory McLane the man.

Abby didn't seem to fit in that group at all. If anything, she'd given him the space he'd asked for and then some. She hadn't even pretended to be thrilled at the idea of having his daughter around, and although it seemed to be working out, he'd appreciated her bald honesty.

But now that door stood open like an invitation. For Regina he was sure, because he had noted how little intimacy Abby had seemed to want with him. Oh, he could occasionally see sexual response in her gaze, but just as quickly she would wipe it away.

Which was what he ought to be doing. She wasn't made for his life, the kind he led back in Nashville and on the road. But not many were. She'd been hurt enough, and he didn't need to add to that.

And maybe he was romanticizing the whole damn situation. She'd survived some real ugliness, and while he felt the tension, the sorrow, the anxiety in her at times, she was doing a fine job of carrying on. A tough woman in her own way.

Apparently he'd stood there too long. Her door opened wider and she peered out from the darkness within. He could see that she was wearing a gray fleece sweatshirt and pants, with socks on her feet. Her dark brown hair was down and tousled.

"Is something wrong?" she asked.

"Caught by a thought," he said. "Just standing here thinking."

He watched her bite her lower lip, and wished he could do that. Idiot. Stop now. But the hunger for her just kept thrumming in his veins.

Finally she said with a tentativeness that troubled him, "Bring your coffee in?"

He looked down at the mug he still held, then walked toward her. Maybe she needed to talk. God knew, sometimes he sure did. The problem was knowing who you could trust. He didn't share much of himself anymore, except in his music. It was the only place that was reasonably safe.

He hadn't really seen her little apartment, but it was nice enough if you weren't hungry for a lot of space. She switched on a lamp, low light, and settled into a yellow-upholstered rocker, leaving the love seat to him.

"You happy with this?" he asked, indicating the apartment with a wave of his hand.

"Very much." Her smile seemed shy, which surprised him. He thought she'd been getting past that.

"Good. I told the lady I wanted a retreat that a woman could enjoy while she was stuck here."

"Stuck?" She surprised him with a small laugh. "Hardly stuck. You give me an awful lot of freedom."

He returned her smile. "I'm glad you feel that way. I know I need help, but I don't have to be mean about it. And here I am intruding on your private time again."

She shook her head, almost too quickly. "I don't feel that way. I wouldn't have asked you in. I was reading in bed, but I couldn't concentrate."

"Why not?"

She hesitated visibly. "Well…it's a huge favor I'd like to ask."

"Ask away." As usual, he felt his defenses start to slam into place, then reminded himself that he didn't know he'd need any with this woman. Nothing she'd done so far would seem to indicate it.

"Well…" Again she hesitated, then tipped her head shyly until she was hiding behind her hair.

He wondered just what hell she had been through to make her reluctant to ask for something. That just plain wasn't right. "I don't bite," he reminded her. "And I am familiar with how to say no."

A sigh escaped her. "I couldn't concentrate because that song you played earlier is running through my head. I'm sure you don't consider it finished by any means but I was wondering… Could you make me a recording of it? The way you played it on the piano? I promise not to let anyone else hear it."

His chest swelled. Whether she knew it or not, she had just paid him the best compliment in the world. She had been touched by something he'd created, enough to want to keep listening to it. That was better than any award by far.

"Sure," he said. "And that's the nicest favor anyone's ever asked of me."

"Really?" Her head lifted. "But people love your music. Obviously."

"But nobody before has ever wanted a personal copy of a hardly finished piece. So I'm honored." He thought he saw her blush, but in the dim light he couldn't be absolutely sure.

"Thank you," she said quietly, then smiled. Really smiled. He felt like he was seeing her for the first time.

"Abby?"

"Mmm?"

"Can I get a little personal?"

Her smile faded, and he was sorry to see it go, but he needed to know more about this woman. She was invading his thoughts more and more, and maybe if he got some questions answered, his curiosity might ease. At least he supposed it was curiosity. Sexual desire didn't have any deep questions, it just was. A natural, innate reaction to a beautiful woman. Somehow he needed to put all this to rest in his own mind, because if this kept up he was going to be thinking about her more than his music.

"Can I refuse to answer?" she asked.

"Of course. I also understand the word no."

A nervous, quiet laugh escaped her. "Okay, ask away."

"I just want to know more about you. I get that you went through a bad divorce. But that can mean a lot of different things. I would have tap-danced when Stella left me, except for Regina. You don't feel like that."

"No," she admitted. "I was hurt. Very hurt." She looked away. "Sometimes I tell myself they deserve each other, but it doesn't help. It was so humiliating, Rory. Painful and humiliating."

"Why humiliating?" He tried to ask gently, not wanting her to think he was judging.

"Because we were married only a couple of years. Because he was carrying on behind my back with my boss. Because I think everyone in town knew except me. Because people can still hardly look at me. Because I feel like there must be something terribly wrong with me for him to do that."

It came out of her quickly, as if a dam had been breached, and he sat there quietly, wishing he could ease her pain somehow. What she'd been through was a helluva lot worse than what he'd experienced with Stella. Had Stella cheated on him? Of course she had. He'd never doubted it. After Regina was born, and when she became secure in her own successful career and no longer needed his help to keep rising, he'd have bet she had quite a few lovers. The temptations in their business were huge, and being on the road so much provided countless opportunities.

He figured Abby's ex and her boss ought to be the ones feeling humiliation, but apparently that wasn't the case. "I don't know why you blame yourself for what *they* did."

She looked at him again, and the hollow pain in her gaze reached out and squeezed his heart. "Because something must be wrong with me. I must have been an awful lover, or an awful wife. I mean...we were only married a couple of years!"

Oh, boy. He stared down at the mug in his hands, facing her honest pain, wanting somehow to ease it, but sure there wasn't much he could do. She seemed to have fixated on her own failures, which he suspected had little enough to do with it.

"Did you cheat on your wife?" she asked.

The question startled him. They were talking about her, not him. But then he made a connection and decided to be blunt. "You've been awfully sheltered."

"Sheltered?" A note of anger crept into her voice.

"Sheltered," he repeated firmly. "Nothing wrong with it. You'd be shocked by the world I live in. No, I never cheated on Stella."

"See?"

He shook his head sharply. "Let me finish. I was pretty experienced by the time I married her. I sowed my wild oats beforehand. You know what that means, right?"

She nodded, her face still pinched.

"I had my share of affairs and even one-night stands. Maybe more than my share. I had women throwing themselves at me. It went to my head. And besides, I'm just a man. Just flesh and blood. I gave in to temptation and I'm not proud of it. But by the time I married Stella I was really ready to settle down. I wanted the whole family gig, and I wanted it to work. All that other stuff... I woke up one day and realized to my very core that it was unsatisfying. Nothing but a pure ego stroke.

I even got a little upset with myself for behaving like a bull in a pasture full of cows. But yeah, that was over and done with when I decided to marry Stella. I didn't want it anymore. I needed something deeper."

She absorbed his words but her pinched look didn't go away. "Porter running off with Joan was a little more than wild oats."

"Probably. But his getting involved with her to begin with was probably exactly that. How old was he when all this started?"

"Twenty-four."

"So he probably hadn't finished sowing his wild oats. I'm not talking about your boss here. I don't know her and she's not what's making you feel so bad. Porter made you feel like a failure. All I'm saying is maybe he started off thinking with his small head. The thrill of it all. Something new and different. I walked into that honey trap more than once. It's easy enough. Guys are especially weak about sex."

"But when you got married…"

"Slow down," he said gently. "I told you I was done with all that. I sometimes even felt sick about how I behaved. But it was the newness and freshness of it all that sucked me in as much as anything until I realized I was being an ass. One morning I woke up, literally one morning, looked at the stranger in bed beside me, and I wanted to scrub my soul clean. That's the only way I can describe it."

Something in her face softened. "Wow," she murmured.

"Yeah. I had an epiphany at twenty-eight. About time I grew up." He knew he was smiling a bit, but he wasn't at all amused with himself. "A good thing it happened, too, because next thing I knew, Stella was pregnant with Regina and I was more than eager to settle down."

She nodded, but lowered her head again, hiding behind that soft brown curtain of hair. He wished he could brush it aside and see her pretty face, but touching her even in such a simple way would be a huge mistake. He was her boss, her employer, and he wanted her right now until he ached with it. He wanted to show her that the only bad lovers were those who weren't loved properly. Not his place, and all the more dangerous because she worked for him. He might want her, but he wanted her to come to him freely, and he didn't want her to feel trapped by her need for work into something she didn't want.

Besides, everything else aside, he felt trust had been burned right out of him. The only person he trusted anymore was Regina. Everyone else wanted something from him, and he had no way to be sure Abby wouldn't turn out the same, one way or another. Nice lady, but what did he know about her? Zip.

So he kept talking. The only thing he could do for this woman was try to reassure her a bit and hope she started seeing things a bit differently.

"Some guys," he said, "can marry young. My dad did."

He had her attention again, and the curtain of hair slipped away.

"Really?" she asked.

"Twenty-one when he married my mom. They're still married."

"Where are they?"

"Living in Jamaica, if you can believe it. That surprised me. All their lives spent here on a ranch. Then I send them on a vacation, and the next thing they're talking about wanting to retire to Jamaica. At least I could help with that. But they were faithful all along to each other, and they sure didn't raise me to act like a rutting bull. I guess that's why I was capable of feeling some shame eventually. But I'm trying to get to Porter here. He was young. Some guys grow up faster, some don't. Apparently he didn't. Men are like a bunch of cats. Dangle something shiny and new in front of them and they want it."

At long last, he drew a small smile from her. "I like that," she said.

"It's true. So here's Porter, living the steady life with a pretty wife. Ought to be grateful. Instead something shiny and new dangles herself his way. He starts off thinking, what can one time hurt? Abby will never know. Well, apparently, it didn't end with one time. I'm real sorry about that, Abby, but Porter did you wrong, not the other way around."

"But I..."

"Shh," he said. "You weren't responsible for his decisions. Marriage is a hard job. It needs a lot of work. If he was dissatisfied with you in some way, part of the deal is that he tells you so you can work on it together. Did he ever do that?"

Again she vanished behind her hair, and spoke in a thick voice, "Not until we split."

"Aha."

"Aha?" That brought her head up again.

"Aha," he repeated. "So he justified his own rottenness by blaming you. Typical."

She just shook her head a little, whether in denial

or surprise he couldn't tell. He decided he'd poked around in her enough for one night and stood up.

"I'm going out to the barn to work. I'll make you a disc of that music you want. In the meantime, ask yourself how you were supposed to be a mind reader. I'll bet Porter felt guilty enough to be sweet as punch until he decided to split. I'll bet he never let on he was unhappy with you in any way. But when the time came, he had plenty of good reasons built up in his head to excuse himself. And I'll also bet that most of them weren't even true. Self-justification. We all do it."

He paused just long enough to brush the top of her head lightly with his hand. "Thanks for talking with me. You're a good woman, a kind woman, and attractive as all get-out. A man would be lucky to have your love."

He exited quickly, sure he wouldn't be able to endure listening to her object to a simple compliment. Now not only did he feel protective of her in some way, he wanted to punch Porter in the face.

The man was the rump end of a mule.

Chapter Four

Abby felt as if her conversation with Rory that night had started some kind of internal shift in her. A month later she still wasn't sure what it was. All she knew was that there seemed to be a gradual improvement in how she felt about herself.

Which was not being aided at all by the fact that Rory had once again retreated into his creative fog. He spent all day in the barn. Regina popped in to say hi before heading out to join him, and she was left to her own devices except for dinner, which both Rory and Regina still ate with her in the kitchen, time spent talking mostly about Regina's days and current school activities and gossip. They seemed to have reached some kind of stasis or equilibrium, where each day was like the next.

Rory had given her the CD she had requested, and

sometimes she played it repeatedly while she was cleaning, or browsing the web trying to figure out a future for herself.

But other than that, he seemed to have dropped some kind of bomb into the middle of her emotional morass, then retreated.

She wondered if that as her fault. After all, she'd heard Regina's succinct comments about people wanting things from her because of her father. He probably felt the same. Maybe by asking for the CD she had crossed some kind of line into the taker class.

How would she know?

But regardless, changes were happening inside of her. She made a lunch date with her friends finally, and found the divorce was off the conversational menu. She listened to them talk about their families and their kids and simply felt wistful. She also endured questions about Rory, but refused to answer their curiosity with anything except she didn't see much of him and he seemed like an okay guy.

They didn't believe the "okay" part, not about a man like that who left women all over the country drooling, but they accepted her reticence in good part.

The weekend arrived, and Regina went over to spend it with a friend. Rory remembered the family from his youth, spoke to them about the visit, then on Friday afternoon Regina took the school bus to their place, to be picked up on Sunday afternoon.

Good for Regina maybe, but Abby was surprised at how acutely she felt the girl's absence. Rally had been left behind, and as it dawned on him that Regina wasn't coming home, he became the personification of moping.

Rory hardly emerged from his studio that night, showing himself only once as he took the dog out for a long run. Then back into the barn.

Abby watched enviously, wishing she was part of that club. But she hadn't really been invited inside. Sighing, she retired to her room and tried to bury herself in a book or in the TV. She wasn't exactly surprised that when Rory eventually came back to the house in the wee hours the dog crept into bed with her. This time she hugged him back, falling asleep with her face buried in his fur.

The following morning, everything blew up. Rory came back to the house from the barn and announced he was going back to Nashville. Her stomach started to sink even before he asked, "Do you mind getting Regina tomorrow?"

"Of course not. Is something wrong?"

His expression was furious and tension crackled almost visibly around him. "Oh, yeah. Stella wants Regina back."

Shock rippled through Abby, so strong that for a moment she felt she had left her body. She grabbed the kitchen counter and asked hoarsely, "Can she do that?"

"Maybe. Maybe not. My lawyer had her sign over custody. Signed, sealed, notarized."

"Then…"

He waved a hand. "She's claiming she signed under duress."

The room seemed to darken. "But…why?"

"Oh, I don't know. She hates me? Free publicity from another custody fight that makes her look like a good mama? She's always used Regina like a pawn. Where's the dog?"

"I don't know."

He gave a whistle. Soon paws thumped down the stairs. "We're going for a run. A long one. When I get back maybe I won't feel like smashing something."

Once again she watched man and dog disappear into the distance, but this time it was no easy lope. Rory ran as if the hounds of hell were on his heels.

Over the mountains, storm clouds were beginning to boil. There might be snow soon.

Not knowing what else to do, Regina put on her oldest T-shirt and bleach-spotted jeans and went on another cleaning binge to work off her anxiety. This wasn't fair, not to Rory nor Regina.

But fairness, she reminded herself, was rarely part of life.

Man and dog returned two hours later. Abby heard them and went to the top of the stairs, her hands still in rubber gloves. "Rory? Are you okay?"

A minute later he appeared, still wearing his jacket. "Sort of. At least I don't want to kill something. What are you doing?"

"Cleaning. You run, I clean."

Just the merest hint of a smile crossed his face. "Cut it out and come down and join me."

So she put away her cleaning supplies, hurried to change into jeans and a sweater that didn't smell like bleach and lye and joined him in the kitchen. Tension filled the air, and she felt it all the way to her core. Desperately she wished she could do something, but couldn't think of a thing. All she knew was that she felt a deep pang for him and his daughter.

Rory had just brewed fresh coffee and Rally was busy slurping down a bowl of water. When he finished, he flopped on the floor like a ragdoll, with a thump.

"I think I wore him out," Rory remarked. He brought coffee to the table. "Sorry."

"For what?"

"It's not your worry."

For the first time she felt genuine anger with him. It flared suddenly as if a match had been thrown in dry grasses. "How can you say that? She may not be my daughter, but I care about her and any fool can see she's happy here. What kind of mother would want to pull her out of school just as she's starting to settle in and make good friends? What kind of mother wants to pull her away from a father she clearly loves? I don't know what kind of nannies she had, but Regina is absolutely no trouble at all. Bunch of cockamamy lies, if you ask me."

"And so the battle lines are drawn," Rory said almost bitterly. He sat across from her, drumming his fingers on the table. Only when he did it, unlike most people, there was a rhythm to it as if he were marking the time to music.

"Regina will say she wants to be here," Abby said with certainty, hoping that might be enough. "Even I can see how happy she is."

"Regina doesn't have anything to say about it, really. And regardless, I don't want to drag her into the middle of this if I can avoid it. This is between Stella and me and a judge."

Abby blinked, astonished. She hadn't considered how involved this might become, but then what did she know about these issues? Nothing except a little bit about bitter divorce. "A judge? Really?"

"Well, not yet. Not until a hearing."

"And that's why you have to go back right away?"

He sighed and ruffled his hair. "Hell. No, it won't happen that fast. I just want to *do* something, but racing back this instant won't repair anything. It won't hurry anything. I told my lawyer to find out what Stella *really* wants, if he can."

Another wave of shock passed through Abby. "My God," she said quietly. "You think she doesn't really want Regina?"

"Yeah," he said. His hand fisted on the table, then slowly relaxed. "Of course she doesn't. She never has. Just a cute little girl to appear in pictures with her, so everyone can see Stella has a beautiful daughter and they're so close. Except they never were. From the time that child came home from the hospital she's been cared for by other people. Some of it you can excuse because of Stella's job, but not all of it. Hell, I had the same job and I was able to make time for Regina. Stella never did unless there was a photographer around."

Anger rose in Abby again. She couldn't imagine how that might have hurt Regina over the years. Eventually she must have noticed and felt it. No wonder she had wanted to come here. She wished she could wrap the girl in a tight hug and never let go. "Unreal."

"Nothing about Stella is real except her ambition, as I learned to my everlasting sorrow." He cussed, leaned forward on his elbows, then leaned back as if he was having trouble holding still. "Sorry I'm so agitated."

"It's okay. I'm pretty agitated, too."

He smiled mirthlessly. "You're doing a pretty good job of playing mama bear."

"I'm not playing," she said hotly. "I told you, I care about Regina. It's plain as anything she loves being with you and she's settling in here. Why rip all that up?"

"Good question." He closed his blue eyes for a minute, and she could almost see him uncoiling. Forcing himself to relax. She wished she knew how to do the same. Certainly, her pain for him was matched and perhaps exceeded by the pain she felt for Regina. Imagine knowing your mother didn't really love you. How did you deal with that?

When his eyes opened again, the flares of anger in them seemed to have damped. "I've got to figure out what she wants. There's something, and it isn't Regina. Publicity? Always possible. But this could turn into a very ugly kind of publicity for her."

He looked out the window. "Storm's coming."

"I saw. Snow, maybe."

"If I don't fly out of here now, I'm not going."

"So hurry up."

His gaze came back to her and he shook his head. "I'm not going. Regina will want to know what's going on, and I don't want her to know. Besides, nothing can happen immediately."

Impulsively, she reached across the table and took his hand. The warmth of his skin reached out and ran through her like hot molasses. She wanted it to go on forever, then silently castigated herself. Awful timing for such feelings, given what was going on. "I'll swear out a statement saying she's happy here."

He turned his hand over and gripped hers. "Thanks, but I don't think the word of someone I employ will have a lot of weight in this. No, I'll have to go at this another way."

"How so?"

But he didn't answer immediately. He stood, stripping his jacket and revealing a dark blue western shirt that was tucked into his jeans. Even in her distress she couldn't ignore the raw masculinity that seemed to emanate from him. An alarm bell tried to sound in her head, but it was strangely muffled.

"You ever heard of a war of attrition?" he asked.

"Vaguely."

"He who lasts the longest wins. Take no prisoners, and all that."

Her heart skipped. She didn't know if she liked the sound of this. "What are you going to do?"

"Nothing I don't have to. Let me put it this way. I'm far more successful than Stella's ever been. Last time I tried to play fair, and I'm still furious that the judge was so biased against men. This time I'm not counting on justice to be blind. She wants a fight? By the time I get done, she and her lawyers are going to be in the poorhouse."

Then he grabbed the cordless phone, punched in a number and went out to the living room. She could hear him talking and soon gathered he was speaking to his lawyer.

Man, she thought, she wouldn't want to get on Rory's bad side. On the other hand, trying to take his daughter away? Maybe Stella deserved everything she got.

By early afternoon, the sky had grown leaden and the wind was blowing strongly enough to rattle windows and keen around the corners of the house. No rain or snow yet, but there was little doubt there'd be some.

Abby made them both sandwiches, and Rory ate his with one hand while he continued pacing and talking with his lawyer. A lawyer who was available on Saturday. She supposed that said something else about Rory's power in the world. Or his nature, that his lawyer would work for him on weekends. They actually sounded like friends and allies from what she could hear.

Not that she tried to listen. It was really none of her business, and she guessed Rory would tell her what he wanted her to know. She put in her earbuds, stuffed his CD into the player on the laptop and listened to that haunting melody to block out what was undoubtedly a private conversation.

She paused to make another pot of coffee, to fuel whatever he was doing, and he gave her a faint smile and a thumbs-up. She managed to return his smile and went back to blindly surfing the web. She was here if he needed anything. Much as she hurt for him, it seemed to be all she could do.

She was feeling helpless again, the way she had when Porter said he was leaving. Nothing she could do or say would change a thing.

A couple of hours later, out of the corner of her eye, she saw Rory replace the cordless set in the charger. She quit pretending she was fascinated by something online, pulled out her earbuds and looked up. He seemed to have relaxed quite a bit, but still had an air of determination as he poured more coffee for both of them.

"Any better?" she asked.

"Much. Do you want the dirty details?"

She hesitated, then tried to joke, hoping to leaven his mood. "As long as it doesn't involve contract killings."

He actually laughed. "Good one. No, it doesn't. But the digging has begun."

"Digging?" She closed the computer and pushed it to the side. "As in?"

"As in I've known for a long time about some of the things Stella does on the road. Drinking, drugs, sleeping around, stuff like that. Whether she knows it or not, even her roadies gossip. A good reason to behave yourself whenever you're not completely alone."

Abby drew a sharp breath. "And *I* felt exposed after the divorce."

"Nothing like I could expose about Stella."

One question rose to the forefront of her mind, one that battered her for an answer. She needed to know about Rory. She hesitated, biting her lip, then dared to ask, "But you don't do those things?"

"Not since I had my epiphany. So for me, you have to go back to before Regina was born to get any dirt. For her you only have to go back to last month. Do you think I'm loathsome?"

She thought it over. On the one hand, it didn't sound like a nice thing to do. On the other... "No. Not if it will protect Regina."

He nodded. "That's how I feel. Anyway, it's not my

intent to expose her. When we divorced, my lawyer insisted I get some private investigators. They got a thick file on her, but I refused to use it. So my lawyer is going back to the investigators to get all the new stuff in sworn statements in case I need them."

"And then your lawyer will threaten her?"

Rory shook his head. "He can't do that. It'd be extortion. I can't exactly do that either for the same reason. But there are ways to let her know that we know without demanding anything. We go public with it only if we have to prove in court that she's unfit."

Abby thought it over, amazed by the tortuous reasoning. "A threat that's not a threat? I don't exactly get it."

"Neither do I. Basically my lawyer said that he'd just let her people know that he's trying very hard to convince me not to take this information to court because it would be bad for Regina." His face darkened. "And it would. God, that's why I didn't do it before. I didn't even mention it. I hope to heaven she's smart enough to back off."

His hands clenched and whatever relaxation he'd achieved vanished in an instant. "I hate this. I absolutely hate this. I don't want to let Regina go back to her and that lifestyle because she says she was miserable, but I don't want to drag my daughter's mother through the mud."

Abby understood his feelings. It wasn't difficult. On the one hand he needed to protect his daughter. On the other, he might have to do something awful in order to protect her. Rock and a hard place of a kind she could scarcely imagine. "You know," she said finally, staring at the tabletop, "from the outside looking in, you seem to lead a charmed life."

He gave a short bark that didn't quite make a laugh. "Right. I know."

"I guess everyone has problems, huh? And this is an especially hurtful and ugly one. I wish I could help."

"You have. You listened. And you didn't tell me what a dog I am to even consider what I'm considering."

She met his gaze. "It's ugly, yes, but I can understand wanting what's best for Regina. You didn't put yourself in this position."

"Didn't I? I got Stella pregnant and married her. I was just too besotted to know the trouble I was buying."

She rested her cheek in her hand, looking into herself, as well. "Aren't we all?"

For the first time that day, he genuinely smiled. "Point taken."

"Sometimes," she said quietly, "when I'm really, really honest with myself, I know that marrying Porter was a mistake. I dropped out of college, I'd only known him a short time and I was too much in love to wonder about the kind of man he was. And in those really honest moments I realize that the signs were there."

"Such as?"

"He didn't always treat me very well. He wasn't abusive, but he *was* selfish. I always excused it. But one of my girlfriends said something a few years ago when she was dating that made me think...although not hard enough at the time. But I think about it now."

"What was that?"

"That she wanted a man who thought the sun rose and set in her eyes. I thought it was a silly, romantic notion, but looking back I think she had it right. It won't be like that every single minute, but it should be like that at least some of the time."

He stood abruptly. "Willing to brave the weather with me?"

She stared at him. "What?"

"Come out with me to the barn. What you just said… I need to noodle around an idea. If you don't mind."

She gathered up her cold-weather gear, figuring that working on his music might soothe him. He needed some soothing. So did she, come to that. She'd been hurting for herself for so long now it was surprising that she had anything left to feel for someone else's anguish. But feel it she did. Her own problems seemed awfully trivial compared to this. After all, she'd only lost a lying, cheating husband and her self-esteem. Rory could lose his daughter, and Regina could be taken from the father she clearly loved. That put Porter's conduct into cold perspective and made her own reaction seem small and maybe even petty.

Yes, the man had hurt her. Yes, he'd shamed her. Yes, he'd said horrid things about her. But that was a far cry from taking her child. The things Porter had taken from her could be regained if she'd just stop wallowing. Rory and Regina were in a very different position.

She met Rory on the back porch and saw that snow had begun to fly. The wind whipped the ends of her wool scarf around.

"I'm reconsidering," he said. "Maybe it would be best for you to stay here."

Her heart plummeted. The last thing in the world

she wanted right now was to be alone with her own thoughts. She'd spend the whole time working up a real head of steam and worry about Regina. And she might as well admit she wanted to be with Rory, dangerous though it might be.

He continued speaking. "If that snow gets much heavier, we won't need a whole lot of it in this wind to create a whiteout. I love my studio, but being stuck in it indefinitely wouldn't be the most comfortable thing."

"Okay," she said, trying to get her stomach to stop dropping.

He turned his head. "I'll be right back. The main thing I want is my guitar and a digital recorder. Easy enough to carry. You get back inside and stay warm."

He jumped down the steps and loped toward the barn. Rally ran with him. Abby didn't go right inside though, not until he disappeared through the door.

He was coming back. The relief she felt overwhelmed her, idiotic or not.

When she'd gone shopping the last time, she had picked up a few things that she could make dinner with at the last minute, just in case. She decided this was going to be an "in case" day. Rory was wound up on rage, fear and worry, and she was doing only slightly better.

But it was too early to cook, so she went to sit in the living room and wait for whatever came. He rejoined her only fifteen minutes later, bringing cold into the room with him along with his guitar case and a small digital recorder.

He set the case beside the piano, and after wiping

the recorder he placed it on top. "This'll probably be boring," he said frankly. "You don't have to hang if you'd rather do something else. When an idea first starts emerging, it can bounce all over the place."

"Okay," she answered, though she felt no desire to do anything else. She'd been welcomed into his creative process for the second time, and she didn't undervalue the invitation.

To her surprise, he didn't immediately bring out his guitar. Instead he sat at the piano and began running his hands lightly over the keys, a rippling waterfall of sound. But then it changed. As if the anger in him took over, the room was suddenly filled with loud, discordant notes. She could feel the rage and discontent and shrank a little in her chair as the music nearly battered her.

She didn't object, though. He was lucky to have such an expressive outlet. She could have used a few of her own, ones that would release her pain and anger without harming anyone. Sometimes she wanted to break something, but even as the urge surged in her, she swallowed it. Rory wasn't breaking a thing, but he was sure expressing the desire to.

As abruptly as it started, it ended. The notes quieted down, lost their discordance, began to slide away into something gentler. He spoke as he played.

"Do you trust like you used to?" he asked.

"No," she admitted. "It's only now that I'm starting to trust my friends again."

"Why did they lose your trust?" Notes kept spilling from the piano, beginning to reach a melody that was pleasant to the ears.

"Because I think they knew what Porter was doing and didn't tell me."

He nodded and played for another few minutes. Occasionally she got the feeling that he had stopped some through-line in the melody and started in a slightly different direction. "What would you have felt if they told you? Would it have helped?"

She felt the vise of old grief grip her again. "I don't know." All of a sudden it seemed hard to breathe, but she didn't want to let her own pain resurface. Rory had more important things on his mind, justifiably so.

"I don't know, either. But maybe they thought they were protecting you. Maybe they thought Porter would cut it out and return to you. Why hurt you unnecessarily?"

"That's possible," she agreed.

He glanced her way as he continued to summon notes from the keyboard. "It's possible," he repeated, his blue gaze intent. "It's even likely if they're good friends. But that doesn't change the trust issue, does it."

"No." She sucked air, hoping to ease the tightness that threatened to suffocate her.

"Betrayal is a hard thing to get past," he remarked, returning his attention to something only he could see. Now he seemed to be feeling his way through the music he played. Notes sounded more tentative. "When it's one or two people, you stop trusting *them*. When it's a whole lot of people, you stop trusting everyone."

That was so true. She drew another shaky breath. "What about you?" she asked.

"I find it hard to trust anyone anymore. A few people I've known for a very long time, but most people? Nah." He shook his head a little, and the music changed again. "That's one of the ways I've changed since I left here, and I'm not real happy about it. I don't think I can ever get back there though, to that boy."

Now the quality of her pain changed. She ached for him yet again. So much lost innocence in this room, and she suspected he had lost more than she.

Presently he spoke again. "There've been people in my life that I really cared about. Deeply." The music took a more somber tone. "Then one day they did something beyond the pale. It sometimes amazes me when I look back to realize that it's possible for your heart to go utterly cold and empty. For love to turn to complete indifference in an instant. I can't explain it any better than that. It's like something dies between one moment and the next, and you know it'll never resurrect. It's gone for good."

"I could use a bit of that."

He glanced her way. "Still pining for Porter?"

"No."

"Then maybe it happened. Maybe it's not love for Porter that's got you tied up in knots. Maybe it's the other stuff."

She thought that over and realized he was right. If she closed her eyes, she could think back to the shaft of agony that had speared her when he told her he was leaving. But she also remembered something else, the moment when everything inside her turned cold as ice. The instant when she had ceased to love him. It had happened fast, and soon vanished in all the other pains she dealt with, but her love for that man had been gone. In that instant, their argument had ended. She had stopped trying to hang on to him. Stopped arguing with his insults.

She had ceased to care. She had turned from him and walked into their bedroom and begun to pack. Yes, the things he said haunted her because she feared they might be true. Yes, she felt humiliated and betrayed in front of the whole world. Yes, future dreams had gone up in smoke. But Porter? There wasn't a cell left in her that gave a damn about him.

She opened her eyes and realized Rory was watching her. "You okay?" he asked.

"Thank you. You're right. It died, and it died fast when it did."

He nodded and returned his attention to the piano. "Feel freer now?"

She did. She couldn't explain what had just happened. Maybe all the humiliation and anguish she'd been through hadn't come from still loving Porter. Maybe it was, as he'd said, other stuff. And if that was the case, she felt that she'd be able to deal with it better if she didn't tell herself she was still carrying a torch. Whatever grieving she was still doing, it wasn't over Porter.

"Always amazes me when that happens, when I realize someone's been cut out of my heart forever." He stopped playing. "I want some coffee."

"I'll get it."

"We can both go get it. I need to move, and I wouldn't be surprised if you do, too. Sitting around listening to me noodle a piano isn't exactly exciting."

"I wouldn't say that," she answered as she stood. "I feel like I've been over all kinds of mountains and valleys of emotions. I knew music was evocative, but I've never experienced it like this."

He gave her a half smile. "It was hard on the ears at first."

"You were angry. I was thinking how lucky you are to have a way to express it. I sometimes want to smash things."

"Do you?" he arched a brow.

"Never. What's the point?"

He laughed quietly and they walked together into the kitchen. "And I never got around to working on that idea that was coming to me after we talked earlier. But it's still tucked in the back of my brain. It'll come when it's ready."

She looked out the kitchen window and realized that snow had taken over the day. It was dark out there, and the mountains had utterly disappeared. Rory filled their mugs, but before they could move, the phone rang.

Abby automatically started to move toward it, but Rory grabbed it first. "Maybe my lawyer," he explained.

Then she heard him say, "Regina? Are you having a good time?" Silence, then in an anger-laced voice, "She called you and said what?"

Abby took her cup and went to her apartment, leaving the door open a few inches. She desperately wanted to know what had happened, but figured she had no right to be nosy. Despite all that Rory had shared with her that day, she needed to respect whatever privacy he chose to maintain.

She turned the rocker around so she could look out her window, marveling at the way the entire world seemed to have disappeared. Except for a telephone, it might have stayed gone for a while.

But reality had come back, apparently with a bang.

Sighing, she sipped coffee and tried to think about what Rory had said about love dying, and about how facing that had indeed freed her somehow. She wasn't dealing with Porter anymore. She was dealing with demons of her own design.

Which meant she might be able to do something about them.

A little while later, she heard a quiet knock on her door. "Come in."

"Do you mind?" he asked.

She swiveled the chair around. "I've been trying not to chew my fingers down to the knuckles. Is Regina all right?"

"For now." He carried his coffee, too, and sat on the love seat. "You're a great person to talk to, Miss Abby. I hope I'm not driving you nuts."

She shook her head and smiled. "I like that you can talk to me. That I can talk to you. I haven't been doing a lot of that, or listening, either, I guess. I kind of closed up on everything."

Unidentifiable emotions chased across his face. "If you'd rather not get involved…"

"I'm already involved. I care. So there."

Again he gave her that half smile. "So do I," he said quietly. "Now for Regina."

"Let me guess. Her mother called her."

"Got it in one." He leaned back, splaying his legs, and rested his mug on one denim-covered thigh. Again the picture of perfect masculinity, but right now she had bigger things on her mind. "She told Regina she's taking her back."

"Oh, no!"

"Oh, yes. Regina was pretty upset, but I managed to calm her down. I offered to come get her, but she decided to stay. Other than that call, she and Betsy Nash are having a lot of fun."

Abby relaxed a shade or two. "So she's really all right?"

"For now. I convinced her that this time I was going to win no matter what her mother did. The devil of it is that she believes me."

An icy trickle of shock ran through Abby. "Don't you believe it?"

"As much as I can." He closed his eyes briefly, but when they snapped open again they looked like twin gas flames. "You can get kicked by a mule just so many times before you'd be a fool to believe it won't happen again. Worst of it was, she said nasty things about me. Which doesn't trouble me, but it troubles Regina. Then Regina…" He paused. "Damn it! That girl knows more about her mother's carryings-on than any girl her age should. I thought I was protecting her from that crap, but she's heard some of it. If I find out where from…" He let the implied threat go unspoken.

Horror filled Abby. Just from Rory's brief description, she could well understand why he didn't want Regina to know about any of that. He'd walked through fire in the divorce to protect her from the knowledge, and all but lost his daughter. Now he was facing it all over again.

To her surprise, he smiled faintly. "Regina takes after me a bit, I guess. She's ready to walk into a

courtroom and spill it all to a judge. But I don't want
her to have to do that."

"Of course you don't." Moved beyond words, forgetting common sense, reticence, painfully learned
lessons, everything but the suffering of the man facing her, she put her coffee aside and went to sit by
him on the love seat.

When he stretched out an arm and hugged her to
his side, she went willingly, letting her head rest on
his shoulder. He smelled so good, she thought as she
inhaled him. As good as he looked. And somehow
leaning against him this way felt comforting.

For a long time, the only sound was the keening
wind and the rattle of icy crystals against the window glass.

"Some storm," he remarked eventually.

She wondered which storm he meant.

"Regina said her mother claimed I'd forced her to
sign over custody. That I'd threatened her. Regina's
not buying it."

"Good."

"I guess she knows Stella even better than I thought."

"Or maybe she knows you better than you think."

"Maybe." He sighed, tightened his arm around her
briefly, then relaxed again. "I got everything in life
I ever wanted and then some. Now I'm fighting for
the one thing I wanted more than anything else and
it keeps trying to slip away. My kid. She's the only
thing that matters."

Abby dared to slip her arm across his waist, feeling the solid muscle beneath. The desire for him that
she struggled to keep at bay rose swiftly. She pushed
it down, aware that more important matters were on

the table and she needed to give them her full attention. "Then you fight with all you have. Even if it gets ugly." She knew about fighting with everything she had to keep Porter, but she'd failed. She could understand why Rory might fear the same thing. She was lucky in a way, though. As they'd talked about earlier, her heart had switched off. She suspected there wasn't any switch in Rory that would turn off his love for Regina.

He spoke a while later. "Running this around in my head like a hamster on a wheel isn't going to help anything. I've done all I can for right now, so maybe I'd better start thinking about something else. I'm buzzing in circles."

She felt him coiling and decided he must want to move. He hadn't asked her to cling to him this way, although he certainly hadn't rejected her when he'd wound his arm around her shoulders. Finding it surprisingly hard to do, she eased away.

"I should cook dinner," she said. "It's getting late."

"I could do without," he admitted. "So don't go to any trouble. I know I should eat something, but…" He shrugged.

"Nothing fancy," she promised. "I have some stuff in the freezer to make quick meals. My emergency backup plan."

He'd been right about not going out to the barn. It wasn't even visible in the blowing snow now, although it didn't seem to be deepening rapidly from what she could see from the windows…which wasn't much. It was impossible to tell whether there was still light or if night had begun to fall because the snow caught and reflected every little bit of light. The outdoors had become a light gray swirl.

Rory followed her to the kitchen to get more coffee. Just as he appeared to be going back to the living room, the phone rang. He snagged it immediately, said hello, then passed the phone to her. He was frowning faintly. "Regina wants to talk to you."

Oh, that couldn't make him feel good, she thought as she held the receiver and watched him disappear into the living room. She raised the receiver to her ear. "Hi, Regina. What's up?"

"Did Dad tell you what's going on?"

"Sort of." Her heart began to tap nervously. She had no place in the middle of this, no right to say much to the girl, and Rory would have every right to get furious with her if she said the wrong thing.

"Well, I'm going to be turning my cell phone off because I don't want my mom calling me again. Let me give you Betsy's number in case he needs to call me."

"You couldn't tell your dad?" Abby wasn't sure she liked this. What was going on?

"Oh, I could have, but mainly I wanted to ask you something he wouldn't tell me the truth about. Is he okay?"

Regina's concern for her father touched Abby deeply. She closed her eyes a moment, appreciating the bond between those two and hoping that someday she'd find the same thing. "He's okay," she said finally. "Furious, worried about you, but okay."

"I kinda feel the same. Do me a favor?"

"If I can."

"Take care of him, Abby. Nobody takes care of my dad."

Oh, wow. After she wrote down Betsy's phone number and hung up, she plopped in a chair at the kitchen table. Nobody takes care of Rory? Astonishment held her riveted. She'd just assumed…

What had she assumed? That people who worked for him could provide the kind of caring only family or really close friends could? And for a man who had learned to be suspicious, how little real comfort could he find?

She heard Rally come into the kitchen, and got her head together enough to look at him and his bowls. No food, no water. Immediately she rose to take care of the dog. He'd been moping all day except for his run with Rory, hiding out somewhere, probably in Regina's room where he'd be surrounded by her smells.

She filled the bowls, then scratched him behind the ears as he ate and drank. "I get it, boy. You're lonely. There's a lot of loneliness in this house. But Regina's coming back." She doubted he understood a thing she said, although his tail wagged a little when she mentioned Regina.

She pulled a few things out of the freezer, veggies and a packaged pasta dinner that she knew from experience was good. However troubled they might feel, a meal from time to time was essential.

Then Rally barked. He rarely did so. She turned from the counter to find him looking at her expectantly. Almost at once Rory appeared. "I need to walk him."

"In this?" She looked out the window.

"I won't need to step off the porch, and he'll go

only as far as he needs to do his business. He's not a stupid pooch."

Not stupid at all, Abby thought as she listened to them go down the hallway to the back door. Rory was talking quietly to the dog and his paws began to dance noisily on the floor. He was eager to get out, all right.

The door closed behind them as she began to put the frozen dinner in a skillet to heat. Then, despite the closed door, the noises of the storm, she heard Rory laugh.

The sound did her heart good. Just a couple of minutes later, they came back in.

Rory rejoined her, grinning. "You should have seen that dog. Never have I seen an animal look that offended. One sniff of the air, one blast of the wind and he couldn't hurry fast enough. Guess he's not a Wyoming dog."

She laughed. "Not yet."

"He'll get there." He paused. "What did Regina want?"

"To tell me she's turning off her cell phone because she doesn't want to talk to her mother again this weekend. She gave me Betsy's number."

A troubled expression came to his face. "She didn't think she could tell me that? I'm not too absent-minded to write down a phone number."

Abby didn't know what to say. Would she be betraying Regina's confidence in some way? Would the truth insult Rory? "Well, she did say she couldn't count on you to tell her the truth about how you were doing. I said you were okay."

At that his face relaxed, and he laughed again,

quietly. "Apparently she can't count on *you* to tell the truth, either."

Abby frowned at him. "What was I going to say? That you were madder than all get-out, ready to punch holes in walls and planning a war of attrition?"

"I reckon not." But he was still staring at her, waiting. As if he knew that wasn't all of it. Darn, did she wear a sign of some kind?

She turned to stir the food in the skillet. "Chicken marsala," she said, hoping to change the subject.

"What else?" said Rory. "What aren't you telling me?"

Abby pushed her hair back from her face, wishing she'd remembered to put it up. How was she supposed to answer that?

"Abby, please."

"It's really a little thing," she answered hesitantly.

"Hardly," he said sarcastically. "If it were, you'd tell me. Look, this is about my daughter. I have a right to know."

It was that argument that did it. Maybe he wouldn't like hearing that his daughter believed he needed someone to take care of him, but on the other hand... when she viewed it from his perspective, it was important. He needed to know Regina worried about him. Maybe he could do something about it.

"All right," she said, facing him, spoon still in hand. "She asked me to take care of you. She said you don't have anyone to take care of you."

Rory's face slid through a range of emotions, followed by a quiet cuss word. "My daughter is worrying about *me*?"

"Apparently so." Abby turned back to the stove.

"She doesn't need to do that. I can take care of my-self. At her age she shouldn't be worrying about that."

Abby sighed. She wasn't so old herself that she had completely forgotten being Regina's age. She put down the spoon and turned toward him again.

"She's ten," she said. "Still a child, but slowly emerging into adulthood. She's got a measure of what's going on, she knows it's upsetting you and she can't do a darn thing about any of it. But she can still worry, and apparently she is. It's a sign of how much she loves you."

"Ah, hell," he breathed. "I didn't want her to know about any of this. Damn Stella."

"I know," she said, sympathy welling in her. "I was here. And I will never understand any woman who would drag her child into the middle of this."

She turned quickly back to her dinner preparations, disturbed by how deeply she was getting involved here. She could deal with her sexual attraction to Rory. Nothing would ever come of it anyway. He didn't trust people, probably mostly women, and she didn't trust men, so it was best to ignore it.

Besides, she couldn't possibly be the kind of woman who would attract a man like Rory McLane. He was used to beautiful long-stemmed roses, not women with real curves, women with a little flesh. Not only could this man have his pick of the most beautiful women in the world, he probably had a whole bunch of cute young groupies after him, as well. So why should he even notice her?

She was his housekeeper, an employee, probably mostly part of the wallpaper to him. Yes, he was nice to her, but he seemed to be a nice man for the most part.

She chewed her lip as she popped the frozen veggies into the microwave. She hadn't heard Rory leave, but as music drifted to her from the living room, she was glad to realize she was again alone.

She was definitely getting too involved, and she ought to know better. How many times had she thought one of her biggest mistakes with Porter had been becoming involved so fast? Well, she'd learned a lot from that experience and she'd be wise not to forget it.

Even supposing that Rory ever noticed her as a woman, where would it get her? He'd be leaving here eventually, returning to his old life, and she'd just be so much dust for him to shake off his heels, the way Porter had shaken her loose.

She mustn't mistake the fact that right now he had only her to talk to about things, only her to listen to his music. That was temporary and meant nothing.

Satisfied with her own self-scolding, quite sure she had put her most important walls back in place, she let Rory know dinner was ready.

Then she sat down to eat, leaving it to him whether to join her or not.

Chapter Five

"What do you want?"

The question came at Abby sideways. Rory had knocked on her bedroom door, then walked in as soon as he heard her voice. Startled, she looked at him from the rocking chair, book open in her lap. "What?"

"Do you know what you want? You're not going to be my housekeeper forever."

Was that a warning or something else? Her mouth turned dry as bone. He stood there, hands on his hips, but she couldn't read his face. Too bad that some photographer wasn't here to take a photo of him right now. His fans would swoon.

"Are you firing me?" she finally asked, her voice cracking with the early stages of panic. She *needed* this job.

"What?" Now she could read his expression, and he looked startled, as startled as he'd made her. "No.

Absolutely no. Let me backtrack. Are there things you want in your future? Stuff you want to do, places you want to go. Dreams?"

She let go of a pent breath. Okay, he wasn't firing her. Panic began to ease and her scrambling thoughts settled a bit. "That's a pretty big question. Why?"

"I know it's a big question." He paced the small space for a minute, then finally settled on the edge of the couch, hands clasped, knees splayed as he rested his elbows on his thighs.

"What brought this on?"

"Thinking about who I used to be, that long-lost kid and Regina. It struck me that the most important thing is life is having dreams and goals. It's not the destination that matters, it's the journey."

"Maybe so," she answered cautiously, not sure where he was trying to take this.

"No maybe about it. Take me. I've arrived. Everyone would agree, I'm sure. I've got a room full of awards at home in Tennessee to prove it. Top of my field, successful and lucky. So much more lucky than most." He paused and shook his head. "You can walk into almost any place in Nashville and hear kids with the same dreams I had, most of them really good. Some maybe better than me by far. The question is, will they get their break? Will they hit at the right time and reach the right audience to set the world on fire? Nobody can answer that. It's luck, not just talent."

"And?"

"And nothing. I'm wandering here. Sorry. The thing is, I've arrived by anyone's measure. All it's taught me is what I've lost along the way. What I could still lose. So I got to wondering what the point of it all is.

And thinking about that made me wonder about you, about Regina. I'm sure she's got dreams of some kind beyond having her own horse. But she's probably too young to go far beyond that. Me, I'm thirty-nine. I have a lot of years left, and I'm wondering what I want to do with them. And that made me think of you. You're young yet, the whole world in front of you, but kicked down by a nasty, selfish guy. Are you just marking time, or do you have hopes and dreams?"

The panic began to stir in her again. "I'm still working through that," she said weakly.

He nodded slowly. "Fair enough. But…" He sighed and leaned back. "I'm acting like a crazy man. Sorry."

She didn't think he was acting crazy, but she also thought that maybe he was asking the wrong questions. Clearly he was having some kind of life crisis. Coming out here to the back of beyond to find his music again, whatever that really meant. Maybe his music was a part of his soul he felt he'd lost. And maybe the real question was how Rory was going to deal with all of this, from his life crisis to his daughter and ex-wife crisis. What he wanted out of all this and where he might go with it.

He sat up again, his blue eyes seeming to be lit from within. "Twenty years I've been on this road. Longer if you count the time before I left here."

"That's a long time," she said carefully.

He tipped to one side and pulled a wallet out of his hip pocket. "My dad took a photo of me the day I left the ranch to go to Nashville."

"How'd your parents feel about that?"

"Not happy, but I guess they knew they couldn't

stop me. They were afraid for me. Maybe they were right."

He opened the wallet, flipped a few leaves, then passed her a photo. It was bent, worn, clipped to fit in his wallet. She took it and held it under the lamp. A tall skinny youth holding a guitar in one hand by the neck looked back at her. "You've changed," she said, not knowing what else to say, except that if she'd met that gangly boy at nineteen she'd have found him every bit as appealing, and she wasn't going to say that out loud.

"Yeah." He took the photo back. "My mom used to complain because I was so thin and my legs so long she had to special order jeans for me from Freitag's. All legs, she said, and nothing else."

She smiled at him. "You were cute."

"Debatable." He put the photo away and tucked the wallet back in his pocket. "I had this yen in me, to make music and have other people like it and want more of it. Even if I'd failed I'd have kept right on making songs. It was like it was in my blood."

"Don't you feel that way anymore?"

"Not often. It's like all the gloss, all the advice, all the guidance, other people's wishes…they put a layer over it all. Gotta please the crowds now, not just me. I'm not saying it's bad, but it's different."

"That changes it?" she asked tentatively, trying to understand.

"Yeah, it does. So I come running out here to find that pure creativity again. The kind that just makes *me* happy. I'm lucky to be able to do it."

"Yes, you are."

"But you don't have that same freedom. And I got to thinking, stupid as it may be, that I'd like to know what you hope for. What your dreams are. Maybe they haven't been completely polluted yet by life."

"Oh, I don't know about that," she said, unable to keep a hint of bitterness out of her voice. "I had simple dreams. Family. Growing old together, grandkids on my knee. I didn't set my sights very high."

His expression gentled. "Actually, I think those might be the highest goals in the world. As I'm discovering."

She studied him for a few moments, trying to connect his utterly different experience with her limited one. All she'd ever known was contained in this county. She had no idea what fame and fortune were like and had never yearned for them.

But there was Regina, and she could totally understand his concerns about her, even though she had no children of her own. So what was he reaching for here? She had no truths to offer anyone. When she'd lost her trust in men, she'd lost a lot of trust in herself.

"Sometimes," he said slowly, "it's not enough to reach the top of the mountain and try to stay there. In fact, it can be cold and lonely up there. Not for everyone, I'm sure, but for me, yeah. So that got me thinking about the journey. The incredible satisfaction that comes from every little success and achievement as you climb closer to what you want."

She nodded but didn't speak. He needed to talk and she was more than willing to listen. There was a deep sorrow in this man, she realized. He might have the world by a string, but there was still plenty of sadness in him.

"I was thinking, too, about all the times you fall down and have to pick yourself up and start again.

The moments when you know what you're made of. Those are important, too."

"Yes."

He raised one eyebrow. "You're working on picking yourself up."

She folded her arms, though she wasn't sure why. Was he getting close to something she wasn't ready to face? Or was she scared of sharing herself with him? Probably the latter. Sharing herself had gotten her nothing but trouble.

He waited, then shook himself. "Sorry, none of my business."

"Maybe not," she agreed. "But you're reaching for something here and I don't know what it is. I can't help if I don't understand."

"Funny thing is, I don't expect you to help. I guess sometimes I just need to hear myself say it out loud. I'm messed up. No real reason that I can see. Somebody as lucky as me shouldn't feel messed up about much."

"You keep saying you're lucky," she remarked. "In some ways you certainly are. But in others, not so lucky. I didn't lose a child in my divorce. I just lost my self-respect, and I can get that back. It'll take time, but it's not anywhere near what you're facing right now."

"If that was all of it, I'd agree. But I'm feeling a certain amount of self-indulgent angst, and sometimes it shames me. I owe a lot of gratitude and I know it. So what the hell am I chasing here? My own tail?" He snorted. "Sometimes I disgust myself."

With that he rose and said good-night.

Before he made it out the door, she rose and caught him by the arm. "Rory?"

He looked at her across his shoulder.

"Don't be disgusted with yourself. You're an artist and you feel something is missing. You're trying to find it. That's not self-indulgent, any more than it's self-indulgent for me to nurse my own wounds until I get past them."

He turned slowly toward her. "This day has really messed me up," he said.

"I can't imagine why."

A slow smile dawned on his face. "You're one helluva woman, Abby. I know you got a whole load of hurt inside you, but you can still find some caring for me and my daughter. Ever heard of sexual harassment?"

The question caught her utterly by surprise. "What do you mean?"

"You work for me. I'd be wandering into lawsuit territory if I told you how beautiful you are, how sexy you are and how much I want to kiss you. So I won't say it."

She caught her breath, almost stunned. Then a tight knot formed in her stomach. "You think I'd do that?"

"You'd be within your rights. But no, I don't think you'd do that. I just don't want to make you feel… uncomfortable with me. Don't want you wishing you worked for someone else."

Considering she'd been feeling like a whipped dog for months now, considering he'd just told her something she'd never thought she would hear, not after the way Porter had shredded her, calling her a cow, saying she was a lousy lover and everything else he could think of to hurl at her to diminish her as a woman and a wife. Rory hadn't made her at all uncomfortable. In fact quite the opposite. He'd made her glow inside.

On impulse, she rose on tiptoes and brushed her lips against his. "Is it harassment if it goes the other way?"

When he wrapped his arms around her and drew her snugly against him, she found out that all her imaginings were real. He was every bit as powerfully built as she had thought, his belly was as hard as rock and his arms…ah, the way they hugged her close felt so good she melted inside. Had any hug every felt this good to her?

He bent his head, and his mouth met hers, just a light touching of lips, as if merely testing her response. Her reaction was instantaneous and full of heat. She never wanted this moment to end, not ever. She felt secure in his embrace, safer than she could ever remember feeling, and the heat of desire only added to the moment as it flickered through her like tongues of flame, lapping at her nerves, ready to burst into a wildfire.

But with a sigh, he ended the kiss, caught the back of her head with one hand and drew it to his shoulder. "So sweet," he whispered. "So very sweet."

Almost dazed by the awakenings inside her, swamped by hungers and desires she had tried so hard to bury, she could merely lean into him and try to imprint every single moment, every single sensation on her memory forever. This might never happen again, but she would treasure it always.

Slowly he released her. She wondered if she was imagining his reluctance in the way he let go. At last she couldn't escape the need to step back.

He smiled at her when she dared to open her eyes, then used a forefinger to tip her chin up. "Thank you," he said, and bent a bit to brush another kiss on her lips.

She sighed, wanting to grab him and draw him close, but knowing instinctively that would be the wrong thing to do. For both of them. A night of romantic play wouldn't resolve anything for either of them. In fact, it might only complicate matters. Man, she hated being sensible right then.

"Good night." Then he was gone.

A few minutes later she heard quiet music issuing from the living room piano. Much more peaceful than earlier. Maybe even a bit happy?

But no, she hadn't done anything to make him happy. No point in deluding herself. Too many clouds hung over his head.

Outside, the wind still howled, but night had taken charge of the world. She settled into her chair again, but instead of trying to read, she closed her eyes and remembered those moments in Rory's embrace.

They had been heaven. Maybe tomorrow that would scare her, but right now all she wanted was to savor them.

Rory played quietly well into the night, seeking an answer in the notes that spilled from the piano. He still hadn't reached for his guitar, although it was where his heart ultimately lay.

Yeah, he was looking for something. And yeah, sometimes he felt like a self-indulgent ass. What could possibly be missing when you were at the pinnacle of your career, wealthy enough to pull a stunt like this and walk away for a while and indulge the desire to write your own music, your own story, just for yourself, even if it never turned into anything marketable?

Midlife crisis, one of his friends had suggested. Maybe it was. He was about the age, and he'd been headed in one direction at full-tilt for so long, maybe he'd left some other stuff by the wayside. Possible.

Then there was this mess with Regina. He'd do anything to protect his daughter. If Stella didn't drop this nonsense, he wasn't kidding about putting her in the poorhouse. He'd heard just enough from Regina to know that Stella was a lousy mother. Not that he hadn't already figured out some of that, but before the divorce he'd been able to make up for it.

Now he had to protect his daughter against her own mother. Somehow that just didn't seem right. True, but not right.

And finally there was Abby. The little mouse who'd been looking after his house and, he guessed, him. Imagine Regina asking Abby to take care of him. That troubled him, that his daughter had such worries.

But Abby troubled him, too. She seemed to have locked up a whole bunch of herself. Of course, he could be wrong. Maybe there wasn't much there to begin with. But he doubted it. When she cut loose a bit, he saw sparks of the woman she could be.

Odd how she seemed to reach him. He was no monk, but in his world, beautiful women were everywhere. In a way, he'd gotten immune to what lay on the surface. Abby didn't fit that image at all. Just a bit plump, which seriously appealed to him, a new discovery about himself. Holding her as he had for just those few minutes had taught him that a soft woman was a much more pleasant package to hold than one who was all bones and implants. A very nice armful indeed.

But it would be wrong to take advantage of that. She had plenty of healing left to do, never mind that he was her boss. Right now the boat of his life seemed to be riding rough seas, and he'd pulled her into that far enough.

How much worse if he followed his sexual urges and wound up leaving for whatever reason. He owed her better treatment than that.

But she fueled the bonfires of his sexual desire, more so than any woman had affected him in a while. He guessed he'd gotten jaded along the way. Jaded and distrustful, and while Abby made him feel strong urges he hadn't felt in a while, he wasn't ready to trust.

Maybe because she wasn't ready to, either. Trust needed to be a two-way street.

He played on quietly, seeking the solace that music had always offered him. From his youngest years, when he'd been given a guitar by his grandfather, he'd been hooked on music. Mostly self-taught, but after months of building up calluses on his fingertips, the rest had come naturally. All of it, even the first time he sat down at a piano and learned which keys made which notes. It was in his blood, a talent that must have come from somewhere, although he couldn't guess. The first few years in Nashville, he'd faced his share of difficulties, but they'd been the ones everyone faced: closed doors and disinterest. Living hand to mouth, taking whatever work he could find, just to support his need to play and sing. Then luck had walked through the door one night when he was playing at a small bar, and life had transformed.

He'd had great times, bad times and some learning to do. It'd be nice to think he'd learned the important things, but he wasn't always so sure.

Then had come the nagging feeling that something was missing inside him. Not just his daughter, although he missed her like hell, but something else. The music was no longer answering all the questions in his heart and soul. It was no longer *his* music.

Sometimes he thought he'd become a parody of himself, even as he knew he ought to be on his knees giving thanks that he'd been blessed in so many ways.

He'd come back to his roots, although not exactly. He wasn't spending his days helping his folks on their ranch. He didn't need to anymore. But he could walk out the door and find the other things that had fed him—the mountains, streams, plains. Even the sigh of the wind and the way the tumbleweed rolled, the sounds that it made if you got close enough to hear the swish and crackle.

He couldn't have said how that turned into music, but it did. Wide-open nature somehow made him wide open, too.

Then of course Stella had put her foot right in the middle of it all. Why should he have expected anything else? He wondered what she really wanted, because he was certain it wasn't Regina. The girl was an accessory to her, like a fine diamond necklace. Something to be shown off, then put away.

He stopped playing, drew a deep breath and rubbed his eyes. Not a good time to get angry all over again.

He'd start hammering the keys and wake Abby. Wouldn't do any good anyway.

He ought to get some sleep. Tomorrow he'd pick up Regina and find out what was going on with her. She might be treating this as if it wasn't a big deal, but two things had given her away: turning off her cell so her mother couldn't call and asking Abby to take care of him.

Asking someone to take care of him. That seriously troubled him. He was her father, it was his job to take care of her and she shouldn't have to be worrying about him, not at her age.

Damn Stella.

"Rory?"

He looked over to see Abby in the doorway, still dressed in dark green sweats. He suspected she slept in them, not a bad choice on a night like this when chilly drafts sometimes crept through the house. Like spectral fingers, they touched him from time to time.

Beside her stood Rally, his head lowered, tail down. One unhappy dog.

"Something bothering you?" he asked.

"Rally is miserable. Then you stopped playing and I grew concerned. How are you?"

"Oh, as right as any man can be, under the circumstances. I stopped playing because I was near to pounding the keys again, and I thought you were asleep. Is the dog bothering you? I can take him to my room."

"He might need a walk, but mainly I think he's lonesome for Regina."

He clucked his tongue and the dog came toward him, too slowly. Reaching out, he scratched Rally behind the ears and around his neck. "You're blue, too, boy? Seems like there's a lot of lonesome in this house tonight."

"I had that thought earlier," Abby said. "A lot of loneliness, especially this time of year with the holidays and all. Anyway, I guess I can step out with him if you're sure he'll come back."

"The way it's blowing out there, he won't even want to leave the porch." He shook his head. "Fool dog ain't so foolish, are you, boy? You want your Regina. So do I." He stood. "I'll take him out back. You can go back to bed, if you want, and close your door. I'll keep him with me."

She gave a little shake of her head. "Sleep seems elusive tonight. I was about to break down and have some coffee. You want me to make enough for you?"

He realized he did. Sleep was going to be elusive for him, too. "Thanks."

She gave him a crooked smile. "Is it a couple-of-cups night or a full-pot night?"

He had to smile back, even though everything inside him was aching for something or other. Her, his daughter, the answers to cosmic questions. He could only shake his head at himself. "I think it's a full-pot night, for me anyway."

She went to the kitchen while he walked down the hall with Rally. He didn't do his usual happy dance, either because he was so low or because he could hear what was waiting outside. Rory grabbed his jacket off the peg and stepped into frozen hell.

Snow felt like icy needles. The wind had taken on renewed life. He couldn't blame Rally for snapping at the snow. Whatever helped.

The dog hesitated, then dove off the porch, went a few steps and did his business in record time. No pausing to sniff at anything. He wanted warmth and the indoors tonight.

When they got back inside, Rally darted down the hall to the kitchen. Already Rory could smell the brewing coffee and he followed the aroma straight to Abby. He saw she'd also pulled out some Danish she must have bought at the grocery, and it was sitting on a plate with a knife on the table. She sat in her usual chair.

"When did that machine get so slow?" she asked.

She made him smile. This woman actually made him smile. Another blessing in his life, he supposed.

"Since we got impatient?" he suggested, pulling out the chair across from her.

"I didn't mean to interrupt you," she said. "You can go back to playing. And pound the keys if you want."

He shook his head. "Won't do a bit of good. I need to get used to this state of affairs. No telling how long it's going to take to get Stella straightened out. Some things just don't have quick solutions."

"I hear you." She put her chin in her hand, kind of looking at him, kind of not. As if her eyes kept darting toward him, then pulling away. Had he made her more skittish? He sure hoped not.

Or maybe she was trying not to look at him because she feared he'd glimpse the heat in her gaze. He'd seen it a couple of times, and if there was one thing life had taught him for sure, it was how to recognize when a woman wanted him.

Keeping a lid on his own passions had gotten easier with practice, but Abby severely tested his self-control. He couldn't be around her without a thrumming awareness of her womanliness, and no amount of telling himself to cool it really helped.

Worse, he actually liked her. She was good to talk with now that she'd loosened up some. And despite her initial reluctance to have Regina here, she'd taken the girl into her heart. That couldn't have been plainer after today.

She was genuine, something he'd been sorely missing. Genuine, cute and, as she emerged from her shell, even charming in her own way. He wanted that woman he sensed inside her, the one she had been before Porter had ground her beneath his heel. He couldn't imagine the things Porter must have said to justify his misdeeds, but he'd bet they were all ugly, to have left this woman so often unsure of herself.

Taking a risk, he just came right out and asked. "So what did Porter tell you? That you're not sexy, that you're a lousy lover, a lousy wife?"

She nodded, her lips compressing. "And more. I'm fat, a fat cow. His words."

"He couldn't be more wrong."

Her head jerked a little. "You don't have to be nice to me."

"I'm not being nice. Just truthful. I like your curves. I don't get why women have to look like boys these days."

She chuckled. "What a thing to say."

"I mean, why should a woman fit into a man's jeans? You aren't built that way. Nature didn't intend for a woman to be skin and bone."

"Oh, heavens, Rory!"

"I'm just being honest. I spent a lot of time with women who were trying to diet down to the bare skeleton. Trying to look like runway models. The thing about runway models is they're supposed to be that kind of skinny so they don't interfere with the way the clothes hang. Walking clothes hangers. The women in my industry…well, they're always complaining about how the camera adds ten or fifteen pounds. So? It adds them to me, too, but I'm not living on lettuce leaves. It isn't right."

She caught her breath, still smiling. "Thanks."

"Not necessary. So you'll never resemble heroin chic. That's a good thing. I'd rather cuddle up to a soft armful that isn't always poking me with bones. But it gets even more ridiculous."

She was still smiling and attentive, and he thought she blushed faintly. The coffee finished and she popped up to get the cups, probably trying to ease out of a slightly awkward moment.

But Rory was past caring if it was awkward. Sometimes the truth needed to be spoken.

"Ridiculous how?" she asked when she returned to the table and sat.

"Where's the first place a woman loses weight?"

She definitely turned red now, so she knew.

"Exactly. So they fight off that weight and the next thing they need to do is run in for a boob job. A never-ending circus in the pursuit of some kind of unreal beauty."

"Stella did that?"

"You better believe it. She must be eighty percent plastic by now. Bigger breasts, injections of collagen and lord knows what, plumping the lips, getting rid of fine lines. It's a constant pursuit of an ideal and it's not real."

She hesitated, a faint smile still on her lips. "It seems to work."

"For some. For those who need to be in front of cameras a lot. For those with stupid husbands."

He'd come right back to Porter. She lowered her gaze.

"Think about it, Abby. He married you in the first place. At the time he sure didn't think you were a fat cow…which you're not, by the way. Not even remotely. And so what if you were? Loving you has nothing to do with how you look. It has everything to do with how appealing you are. You're appealing in a lot of ways, and if you finish coming out of that shell he put around you, you'll be even more so. I keep catching glimpses of it."

He figured now might be a great time to shut his mouth. He'd said more than he should have, about matters that she hadn't invited him to comment on.

But then she raised her head again and smiled at him. "You're a sweet man, Rory McLane."

"Maybe I've just grown up. Some at least. The thing is, I live a lot of the time in a make-believe world. Oh, there's real stuff, real problems, real work, but a lot of it is make-believe. I outgrew that, and sometimes I get a real hankering for what's genuine. Sometimes it's hard to tell."

"Hence coming back here."

"Partly. I'm still living in a gilded world, though. I'm sure you've noticed."

She shook her head. "But reality intrudes."

Boy, did it ever. His thoughts returned to Regina. "Yeah, it does," he said presently. "It surely does. Whatever, I'll say it again. The things Porter said to you were excuses for himself. Don't be taking to heart the words of a cheat and a liar."

Her eyes widened a bit. "I hadn't thought of it that way."

"Well, that's what he was. Why should you believe a single word he said?"

Why should she believe a single word he said? The words followed Abby back to her room when Rory returned to the piano. He played softly, quietly, almost a lullaby, and she stretched out in her bed, still wearing her fleece, buried under a comforter as the storm outside knocked at her windows, demanding entry.

A cheat and a liar. In all these months, she hadn't thought of Porter quite that way. She'd been furious with him, hurt by him, ashamed of her own failings. Mad that he'd cheated on her, but blaming herself for her inadequacies. Surely he wouldn't have cheated if she'd made him happy?

That question had plagued her endlessly, along with an unbearable sense of failure and humiliation. But Rory had opened up a man's mind to her in the most interesting way. A man was like a cat, attracted to anything new and shiny. The man wouldn't have married her if he'd really thought she was a fat cow. And why should she believe anything a liar and cheat said?

He'd said she was pretty and appealing, too. She hugged that to herself. From a man like Rory, that meant a whole lot. He could have any woman he wanted, or as near as made no difference. She'd even done something the other day that she wasn't proud of. She'd gone online to learn about Stella. She was a flawlessly beautiful woman, quite the star herself. When she looked at the photos, she could see a slight resemblance to Regina, although in her opinion, Regina resembled her father more.

She had also seen plenty of photos of Regina with her mother. So Rory hadn't been kidding about how Stella used her daughter. She soon gathered that most celebrities tried to keep their children out of the limelight. Not Stella. Funny, though, Rory had a slew of photos online, but only a couple showed him with Regina, and they were outdoors, caught together as they went somewhere. Not posed like the photos of Stella and Regina.

Abby wondered about that. Stella worked so hard to look sexy and tempting. How did her daughter add to that? She didn't get it. But there was probably a lot about that world she didn't get and never would.

Anyway, she felt guilty for even having looked for the woman online. She was getting too far into all of this, and she felt a bit like Peeping Tom. Curiosity and all that, but really none of her business even if it was all publicly available.

Rolling over, she hugged a pillow, remembering a hug, a kiss, and kind words. Heat pooled in her, like a gravitational force, drawing her awareness downward to the warm place between her thighs. Dangerous feelings, but only if she unleashed them, so she let them be, enjoying the reawakening of her femininity after so long. Rory awakened her that way, and in other ways, as well.

But she was still afraid. While everything he said about Porter made sense, she had to accept that she'd been lied to before, as well. The whole time he had cheated on her he'd been lying to her one way or another.

Could any man be trusted?

She wondered, seriously wondered. She watched Rory with Regina and saw something special there, but he was still a man who was capable of threatening a war of attrition against his daughter's mother. She could understand why, but it made her uneasy anyway.

How could she know if he was the kind of man who would do anything to get his way? No way to know, not yet, and she was far from ready to trust him or any other man.

There had been a time not so long ago when she had trusted as easily as she breathed. Taking everyone at face value. But as she was learning, once lost, trust became a hard thing to regain. She'd closed into a protective shell, all right, but for good reason. Opening up meant taking the risk of getting emotionally gutted again.

She squeezed her eyes shut focusing on her need to protect herself. She couldn't endure that pain again.

But as the wind continued to rattle the windows, she remembered what Rory had said just a little while ago to the dog. "There's a whole lot of lonesome in this house."

There surely was. And odd as it might seem, Rory apparently was one of the lonesome ones. Unwillingly, realizing the risks, she nonetheless felt sympathy for them all.

Chapter Six

Rory had fallen asleep on the couch, dog on the floor beside him. Looking in, Abby smiled. Rally raised his head immediately, attentive, and she motioned to him. If Rory could let him out back, so could she.

The sun was shining again, but the snow was still blowing hard, a bright day being lost in a whiteout. She grabbed her jacket and stepped out onto the back porch. Rory was right, the dog didn't like this. He didn't go very far to make his deposit before loping back up to her side.

Even though the day had brightened a lot, the barn was still just a gray hulk behind the blowing snow. Abby knew this kind of weather from long experience, although it didn't usually happen so early in the season. Whiteouts usually waited until the depths of winter when the snow was so dry it didn't take much wind to kick it up. Of course, they didn't usually have snow this early, either. One thing was for certain, they could probably be sure of a white Christmas.

Not that it mattered. Things changed, the weather got weird sometimes. She let herself and the dog back in, then went to start breakfast. As lightly as they'd eaten last night, she decided to break out the bacon.

But first she fed and watered Rally, who seemed a little less blue this morning. His tail had risen to half staff and wagged a bit as she filled his bowl.

"Fickle boy," she said to him as she patted his rump once. "Getting over your best girl already?"

Or maybe resignation was just settling in. The dog stayed with her, begging silently when she started frying the bacon. Oh, he wanted some of that. She wondered if it would be a sin to give him a piece of the real thing instead of one of his bacon treats. Probably. Why spoil him for things he couldn't continue to have?

The question drew her up short for a minute. Was that happening to her? Was she developing a taste for things she couldn't have, like Rory and Regina?

If so, she was headed for a mighty fall sooner or later. Of that she had not the least doubt. Rory would go back to Nashville eventually, and wherever he went, Regina and the dog would go with him.

Loss already shadowed her future, as it darkened her past. Which she guessed made her the ultimate fool.

She looked at the Great Dane, unable to mistake the pleading in his gaze. "Dog treat for you," she said firmly, then went to get him one. No way was she going to teach that animal to want what wasn't good for him.

A lesson she needed to keep in mind for herself. Most definitely.

"I smell bacon."

Rory's voice drew her attention to the kitchen door. She wondered if he had any idea how scrumptious he looked with tousled dark hair, sleep-heavy blue eyes, and his shirt hanging crookedly.

"The aroma of bacon will wake the dead," he remarked. He stepped into the kitchen and she immediately reached for the coffeepot to pour him a mug. He slid into the chair at the table and put his head in his hands.

"To feel this hungover," he mumbled, "I should have at least enjoyed getting drunk last night."

A quiet laugh escaped her. "You're just overtired."

"You're looking pretty chipper," he remarked as he lifted his head when she put the mug in front of him. "Thanks."

"It's all pretense," she answered. She was feeling the lack of sleep, as well, but she would have bet she'd gotten more of it than Rory had. She'd fallen asleep listening to him play quietly.

She flipped the bacon and separated some more slices for cooking. "Are you hungry?"

"Surprisingly enough, I'm ravenous."

"Eggs?"

"Perfect. What can I do to help? Toast?"

"I can handle this, and you're hardly awake. Enjoy your coffee."

"Yes, ma'am." Then his gaze trailed to the phone. "Nothing from Regina?"

"Not yet, but considering she's been at a sleepover all weekend, she's probably zonked by now."

"Yeah." He laughed a little. "I forced myself to get used to not having her around all the time, but that's gone by the wayside. I miss that girl."

"I do, too," Abby admitted. "You know, I can't imagine her driving a nanny crazy."

He smiled wearily. "I can. Stella probably exaggerated the degree, but if Regina dug in her heels and got really stubborn, she might have frustrated one or two into quitting. Especially if they expected unquestioning obedience all the time. My fault. I didn't want my daughter to be raised to be a robot."

Abby continued cooking, wondering how many strips of bacon amounted to ravenous. She liked that he didn't want his daughter raised to be a robot, though. As she was cooking, she noted that the day grew darker, as if fresh clouds had blotted out the sun from earlier.

Then the phone rang and Rory snagged it. "Hello? Oh, hi, Nancy. How are the girls doing?" Silence. "Well, sure, if you think you can survive it." He laughed. "All right then. Yeah, put her on."

Abby quickly pulled bacon from the frying pan and put it on a paper-towel-covered plate. She listened intently as she put more bacon into the pan, then popped some rye bread into the toaster. Butter. She had to remember butter.

She loved the way Rory's voice changed when he talked to Regina. It grew gentle and warm, like a wonderful blanket. He did more listening than talking as she reached for the butter dish and set up her assembly line. Toast for two had become meaningless all of a sudden. Like how many strips of bacon to cook. Sighing at herself, she calculated one slice of toast for herself and four for Rory. If he wanted more, she could make it.

She was pulling the last of the bacon from the frying pan when he hung up. She took the pan from the heat to let it cool a bit before she started the eggs, and turned. "How is she?"

"Oh, she's having a wonderful time. Nancy Nash said to forget coming to get her today. The roads are impassable in places, there's more snow coming in and she says Regina can catch the bus with Betsy in the morning. The girls aren't driving her crazy, and Regina says she's having a wonderful time, and by the way, Betsy has a horse."

Abby had to laugh. "The horse dream is still alive and well."

"Apparently so." He rose and came to get more coffee before sitting again. "I heard all about the horse, and how good Regina is getting at looking after it."

"Thud."

He laughed, the sound tired. "I heard that hint. Probably the whole county did."

"How many eggs?"

"Two, please. Over easy?"

"Done." She turned back to the stove and cracked eggs into the pan that she had put back on the burner.

"I'm thinking about it," Rory admitted. "Thing is, the horse would have to stay here. No place for it at my Nashville home, and transporting it all that way... would that even be kind to the horse? Why do I think that would cause a whole new raft of problems?"

"Because you're smart?"

He smiled wryly. "Or maybe too adult. I don't know. I'm thinking about it and that's as far as I'll go right now. Eventually I'll probably have to go back to touring and all that, unless I want to retire permanently. Not sure I'm ready for that. And if I head back, well…" He shrugged one shoulder.

She put plates full of bacon, eggs and toast on the table and he dug right in. She was a little slower, sipping some coffee first. *When he went back to Nashville.* The words seemed to be written on the air in neon. But how else could it be? He couldn't possibly run a career from here, could he? Everything he needed was there.

"Did you ever want to leave this place?" he asked her as he dipped a corner of his toast in egg yolk.

She wondered why he was asking. Her heart lifted a little. Maybe he wanted a housekeeper back in Nashville? But that would get her nowhere, really. She needed to build a future, and housekeeping wasn't her idea of one. "I'm thinking about going back to college," she offered. "I dropped out to marry Porter."

"Seldom a good idea," he remarked. "Hormones rule, don't they? So what did you want to do? Or rather, what do you want to do now?"

"I'm not sure," she admitted. "My parents' business was failing and I hung on with them until they couldn't make it anymore. Dad found a job in Colorado Springs and I started at the state university in Laramie. Then Porter."

"Porter seems to be a big bump on the road of life."

Again he made her laugh. "Good description. Anyway, I lost sight of everything else for a few years. Now I'm thinking about it again, and much to my surprise, I'm interested in a whole lot of things, even subjects that didn't use to interest me."

He glanced up from his plate, smiling at her. The smile warmed her all the way to her toes, and inklings of hunger for him reawoke. She licked her lips, ignoring the desire. "That's a great position to be in, every door open to you, nothing that's got you too tied down to do what you want."

She nodded. "It feels kind of freeing when I browse school catalogs online. I don't need to make up my mind right away. First I need to save up so I can avoid a lot of debt. Then we'll see." She hesitated. "You're tied down, aren't you?"

"Pretty much." He sighed and reached for another slice of toast. "One of my friends did something I started thinking about after I got Regina back. He settled where his kids were going to school and gave up touring so he could be with them. A man could make a worse choice."

"Would that hurt your career?"

"Can't say for sure. He's going back to touring now they're grown up, and the concerts are selling out. Doesn't mean it'd be the same for me. But if it isn't…" He shook his head a little. "I came back here to start writing my own music again. If I can do that, I don't especially care anymore who sings it. I've kind of lost the taste for performing. That could change, though."

He gave her a crooked smile and touched the back of her hand briefly, a light caress that renewed her desire for him. She couldn't help but imagine being touched like that all over. "One of my friends called this a midlife crisis."

"Is it?"

"I don't think so. Needing a change isn't always a crisis. It's just a recognition that things aren't satisfying in some way. I told you I left here with big dreams. I've fulfilled them. Now I guess I need a new set." He finished his breakfast and rose, carrying his plate to the sink where he scrubbed the egg yolk off it before putting it in the dishwasher. "Look at that. It's blowing up again and getting darker. I guess I ought to see if I can find the weather on one of these dang TVs."

"Why do you have so many?"

His smile was wry. "You'd have to ask the decorator. I almost never turn them on."

He helped with the dishes, then headed back to the living room, telling her to join him if she wanted. After her upset over Stella's actions yesterday, she'd done about all the cleaning she could, so she didn't feel guilty. Unplugging the laptop she'd been using in the kitchen, she went out to the living room, planning to look over some more college websites. Kinda silly she supposed, since she'd need to attend a state college for financial reasons, but looking over the breadth of career options available to her was becoming a little addictive.

Rory wasn't sitting at the piano. He was leaning forward on the couch, holding a battered old guitar on his knee, twisting the keys as he tuned it.

"That looks like it's traveled a lot of miles," she remarked.

"Cracked, worn and still beautiful," he answered. "My granddad used it for years. Then he passed it to me. Great tone, for such an old, battered instrument."

Satisfied, he strummed the nylon strings and nodded to himself. Then he astonished her by playing a flamenco piece. A country musician playing classical music? But it was so upbeat and powerful that she found her toe tapping and the laptop forgotten.

He flashed her a grin as the last notes faded away. "Now all we need is a couple of dancers."

"I love flamenco."

"It's amazing, all right." But now his fingers wandered off into something quieter and more mournful. "I keep remembering what your friend said about the sun rising and setting in her eyes. There's got to be a song in there."

"I wouldn't know. Like I said, I thought it was silly at the time. Not so much anymore, but it's still trite." She sighed. "Trite may not be the best thing for a song."

"Things become trite because they're true at a deep level everyone recognizes. And most of my songs could be called trite."

She felt her cheeks heat. "I didn't mean…"

"Relax, Abby. I didn't take it wrong." Quiet, melodious chords issued from the guitar. "It's like the way folks scorn romance novels, you know? But what are most songs about? Love and romance."

"Lost love," she reminded him.

He smiled. "Yeah. I need to write one where the guy gets the wife, the pickup truck and the dog back."

She laughed. "You are too much!"

"Well, it'd be a change."

Deciding she might be disturbing him, she opened the laptop and began scanning college websites again. She was just beginning to get a sense that she might like to go into nursing or teaching. But there were so many other possibilities out there that she wasn't going to dismiss one of them this soon. Heck, maybe she could even be an engineer. At this point she didn't know where her talents lay, or even her deepest interests.

Except for Rory, of course. Her interest in him just kept growing until he occupied most of her thoughts. Him and Regina. And all that was doing was muddying the waters. She'd been burned so badly by Porter that she'd vowed never to expose herself to that kind of pain again.

Apparently the heart was an unreasonable organ.

She stared grimly at the computer screen, remembering his question about whether she'd ever thought of leaving this area. The truthful answer was no. She'd never felt the call of big-city lights and crowded places. She was a happy little country mouse, it seemed. Well, maybe not happy, but certainly a country mouse.

Soft liquid notes poured through the room, making a promise of some kind, trying to draw forth a whole new series of feelings in her. She closed her eyes and let them flow, filling her with yearnings that had no name.

The music stopped. She opened her eyes to find him staring at her.

"Am I making you blue?" he asked.

"No. It's beautiful. I'm just drifting on it, letting it take me wherever it wants."

He smiled. "Abby, you have an innate appreciation of music. You're not even looking for words, you're going with the flow."

"Do words mess it up for you?"

"Sometimes. But audiences want songs, you know?

The music is a backdrop for most people, and a lot of people don't even realize how bad those same words would sound without the music. Kinda like the movies. You ever seen a film clip with the music removed? More than half the tension and meaning goes out of the scene. Some people create poetry with words. Few singers do. Our poetry comes from the melding of words and music together."

"Music is evocative."

"Exactly. Words can be, too, but most songs wouldn't stand on words alone. That's why I'm trying to get my music back."

"Don't let me get in your way."

"You're not."

He went back to playing. Her computer had gone to sleep, so she hit a key to wake it up. Focus on her future. One thing she was sure about, it didn't lie here with this man.

A couple of hours later, the phone rang. Rory reached for the cordless set nearby and put it to his ear.

"Oh, for pity's sake, Stella," she heard him snap. "The girl's spending a weekend with a friend. If she doesn't want to be bothered, what's wrong with that? And yes, I know she's okay. No, I'm not giving you the friend's number. If you have anything to say, say it to my lawyer."

He disconnected without even saying goodbye, his knuckles white as he gripped the phone. "Of course she's not answering her phone, you witch. Why would she after the stuff you dumped on her yesterday?"

After a moment, he put the phone down, but he also put aside the guitar.

"Damn, I need a walk." A glance at the front window apparently told him how that would be foolhardy right now. Even the most seasoned person could get lost out there.

She sat where she was, listening to him run up and down the stairs a dozen times. Then she heard the sounds of the shower running. Maybe an hour later he reappeared, dressed in fresh clothes, his hair a little damp.

"Fit for company again," he remarked.

"Expecting some?"

"Just you." Then the phone rang again. He glared at it. "Oh, for the love of Pete…" He snatched it up. "Hello?"

She watched him uncoil a bit. "Not yet, Brian. I don't care how much they're offering. I'm on sabbatical and I'm not changing my mind.

"Yeah… Yeah…" He walked into another room. Abby felt almost like an eavesdropper on his life and wondered if she should go hide out in her apartment. But he'd invited her in here, and she sensed he really didn't want to be alone right now. Given what had happened since yesterday morning, she could understand it.

She had thought she had a peck of troubles, but she was beginning to think that she didn't know what real troubles were. She'd been ditched by Porter, who'd said some nasty things. That didn't come close to having to fight for custody of his daughter, or an ex calling to shrew at him or, apparently, a manager who wanted him to start making money again.

When he returned again, the conversation was over. He stood looking at her. "My manager. Apparently I'm passing up a great opportunity."

"You're probably passing on more than one."

"Yeah. And I'm beginning to wonder if coming out here wasn't just a mistake. I'm learning an important lesson all over again."

"Which is?"

"That wherever you go, you take yourself and your troubles with you. Can't escape it."

All of a sudden he crossed the room and squatted in front of her. "Shoot me for a dog, but I want to disconnect the phone and make love to you."

The statement was so bold and unexpected that it left Abby breathless. When she could find her voice she finally said, "Yeah, right."

He lifted a hand and cupped her cheek. "You, Abby. Not just anyone. You." Then he rose and moved away, apparently taking her words as a no.

Her thoughts scrambled like mice trying to escape a hawk, so fast that she couldn't grab on to one. Reactions poured through her in heated waves. Explosions seemed to be going off in her head.

"You're my boss," she said, the one cogent thought that emerged from the morass of longing and fear and hope. Everything else in her had already decided.

"I sure as hell am," he muttered. "Forget I said it. You're safe with me."

"And…and…"

"And what?"

Pain poured from her then. "I don't want to be just an easy escape for you."

"Escape?" He froze, looking thunderstruck. "Is that what you think?"

"You've got a whole lot of things upsetting you. Who wouldn't want to forget for a few hours?"

Something in his face tightened. "I shouldn't have said anything. You're right, I'm your boss and I don't want you to feel pressured in order to keep your job. But I want you to understand something else. Listen to me very clearly, Abby. Really listen."

Her fists knotted, she managed a jerky nod. She'd been fighting this attraction from the start, telling herself she was a fool, that she'd only get hurt, but now here she was hurting herself by arguing against the very thing she wanted, and had wanted even more since their kiss and hug. Why did it all have to be so complicated? Why did she fear a man who been unfailingly kind to her?

Because she didn't trust. Not just him, but men in general. She could lay that directly at Porter's door.

"Are you listening?" Rory asked again.

"Yes," she managed to say. Her heart was thudding in her chest now, a heavy beat full of fear, though she was no longer sure exactly what kind. Fear of being hurt? Fear of being used? Or, bigger yet, fear that he didn't mean what he was saying?

"I've been attracted to you since the first moment I saw you. I also knew you'd been hurt. Do you think I want to add to that?"

Actually, no she didn't. But he might anyway. The real question was did she want him enough to risk it? Sometimes she thought so, but then she'd remember he could have his pick of women, so why should he want her?

"I'm spending more time thinking about you than thinking about my music. Yes, I want you. I'm crazy with wanting you. I think you want me, too. But it has to be more than that, for you especially. You're not a one-night stand kind of woman, and if you were I wouldn't be interested. I had my share of that. And I'm making a mess of this. Just trust me on one thing, Abby, even if you can't trust anything else. I want you all the way to my soul. For real. Just you. And now I'll go up to my room before I scare you into running. You can forget I ever said anything; we'll go back to the way things were. Just don't hit the road. I'd never forgive myself if you felt you couldn't trust me not to bother you again."

She listened to him climb the stairs and wondered what was wrong with her. She sat on, alone and lonely, and wondered how she had become so broken that she found it hard to believe Rory wanted anything more from her than a roll in the hay and a chance to forget his problems for a few hours.

He could have the same worries as she did. He was a famous man with all kinds of groupies living in a world of people who used him one way or another. Why should he trust *her*? For all he knew, she might be looking for a ticket to better life.

He'd asked her about it, hadn't he? Whether she wanted to leave this place, what kind of future she wanted. She had thought that natural curiosity, but maybe he'd been trying to sense if she wanted something from him. Like everyone else.

It was a mess. Two people with plenty of reasons to distrust. He'd been used more times than she could imagine. More times than she had for sure. She had nothing anyone wanted. Except her body, apparently.

That kind of surprised her. Despite his comments about how wrong Porter had been, she guessed she hadn't really taken it to heart. He'd been trying to tell her then how attractive she was.

But was attraction enough? Of course not, in the long run. But why was she looking at the long run? She hadn't even imagined one yet, except for some vague future in which she saved enough money from this job to get her started in college eventually.

Life offered no guarantees. How long was she going to stay curled up in her shell, avoiding everything because she was afraid? There'd be no relationship with Rory, but did that mean she had to deny herself the first thing she had really yearned for since Porter had broken her?

Or maybe she needed to learn to take a risk again. To just live for now, because there was no way to know what tomorrow might bring.

She heard him moving overhead, using the bathroom to wash up, then crossing his bedroom. An experience, a possibility, was slipping out of her hands while she dithered about things that might never happen.

But to trust herself to get into bed with a man again?

Then she remembered all he'd said.

Before she knew it, aching need propelled her up the stairs, swamping rational thought. When she reached his room, the door was open and he was standing in the dim light of one lamp, his shirt off, revealing an expanse of well-muscled chest and strong arms.

His jeans were unbuttoned, unzipped, hanging low on his hips. He'd shed his boots and socks.

Eye candy, some idiotic corner of her mind noted.

Startled, he looked at her. "Everything's okay, Abby. Really."

"No, it's not." Clenching her hands until even her short nails bit deeply, she took a step into the room.

"Abby?" he questioned.

"I don't know if I'm being a fool. I was a fool once before."

He nodded, but didn't try to persuade her.

"You could have any woman in the world," she said, her voice cracking.

"I don't want any woman in the world." The answer was quiet and firm. "And I sure as hell don't want to make your life any harder. I should have kept my mouth shut."

"No." She was glad he hadn't, because in addition to the simmering desire he woke in her, she felt a new glowing kernel, one that seemed to be emerging from the destruction Porter had left in his wake. A sense of self, of worth. Just a kernel, but he'd brought that back to life.

"You…" She trailed off, unsure what to say. Then, "You make me feel like a woman again."

The smallest, gentlest of smiles curved his lips. "No less than you deserve. I'm glad."

"I don't know if this is smart. No promises."

"None," he agreed. "Maybe that's not good for you."

"Maybe that's exactly what I need."

His brows lifted. "How so?"

"Just to be. Just to feel like a woman. Just to know I can please…"

"Aw hell." He crossed the room and pulled her up against him, the skin of his chest warm and smooth against her cheek. "You please me. Already you please me. Are you sure?"

She managed a jerky nod. She was sure she needed this experience. She wasn't sure how she'd feel about it tomorrow, but she *had* to know if she could make a man happy in bed. Porter had stripped that from her, and damn it, she wanted it back.

And she wanted Rory. More than anything else she wanted Rory. Just once. It was like a child's plea. *Let me just once.*

But it was no child leaning into him, lifting her arms to wrap them around his narrow waist. It was a woman trying to be born again.

Rory had had his share of sexual encounters in his life before Regina. Not something he was proud of, and he supposed if anyone ever asked him for an accounting he probably wouldn't remember half of them. But things had changed since Regina and fatherhood, and he felt as nervous in some ways as a young boy.

This woman was strong and fragile at once. He'd gotten a measure of her strength in the way she'd started putting herself back together after Porter, but she was a long way from recovery and the last thing, the absolute last thing, he wanted to do was add to her scars. How would he know what kind of lover he was? Most of the women he'd bedded had been more interested in adding a notch to their belts than in him. He'd been a prize, a trophy for them.

This woman was looking for no trophies, unless he'd totally misjudged her. She needed reassurance as much as anything, and he honestly wondered if he was the man to provide it.

But he'd set this ball in motion, and now she was here under her own steam. The absolute worst thing he could do would be to back away now because he feared for her.

He was a damn fool and knew it, but he also knew how much he'd come to crave her. For weeks it had been building, held in check for lots of good reasons ranging from the fact that she worked for him to his daughter.

But Regina wasn't in the house, wouldn't be again until tomorrow. So that left the other reasons, all of them, rapidly turning to dust as he held Abby.

For a while he just kept hugging her, giving her time and space to change her mind. Holding her as if this filled some kind of hole in him and told him just how much he'd been missing this most simple and important form of human contact: a hug.

But desire was rising in him again as he held her, feeling her soft curves. It wasn't enough to have her pressed to him. He wanted to fill his eyes, his mind, his hands, his mouth with every inch of her. He wanted to feel her tremble and shudder under his ministrations until she cried out for joy.

He wanted to bury himself deep within her and take flight to the stars. To find release in her and give her the same.

His heart was thudding with hunger now, his erection stiffening until it felt almost painful. He could have swept her onto that bed and made love to her in a New York minute. But she needed more than that.

And frankly, so did he.

He ran his hands over the curve of her back, encouraging her to relax even more. He heard a gentle sigh escape her and she burrowed more deeply into his embrace.

"I want to see you," he murmured. Fevered imaginings for the last few weeks were no substitute. She probably had no idea how much she revealed when she donned her fleece and didn't wear a bra. He already knew she had full breasts and rounded hips but those hints weren't the same and definitely weren't enough.

She drew a shaky breath, then eased her hold on his waist. Stepping back, her eyes closed, she started to lift her sweatshirt over her head.

He touched her hands. "Let me."

Her move to undress herself reiterated her decision, but he still moved slowly as he lifted the material, giving her another chance to change her mind. He wished she'd open those lovely golden eyes of hers, but he could understand her shyness.

Beneath the shirt he found smooth skin and more softness. No ribs poking out. As he raised the shirt higher, he found her breasts, as full as he'd thought, with nipples already pebbled and begging for a man's touch and kiss.

"Man, you're beautiful," he murmured sincerely as he tossed the shirt away.

A little shake of her head told him she still wasn't believing it. Maybe couldn't believe it. He grew determined to convince her otherwise. He cupped her breasts in his hands. Firm. Soft. Real. And yeah, he could tell the difference.

"Abby. Open your eyes."

"No…"

"Please. I'm admiring you. You shouldn't hide from that." In a few more minutes he doubted he'd be able to talk at all. The throbbing in his loins was beginning to reach his brain, a primitive drumbeat that wanted to overcome reason. He fought it back. For now.

Her eyelids fluttered, then at last they opened a little.

"Look down," he said.

Hesitantly she did.

"See how beautiful your breasts are? I'm holding them, and love the way they look and feel. Woman, you are perfectly endowed."

She surprised him then with a wry comeback. "You'd know."

At first he felt a flicker of anger, but it was quickly swamped in other realizations. "Yes, I would," he said. "This ain't my first rodeo. Keep that in mind."

Then he brushed his thumbs over her engorged nipples and heard her sharp intake of breath. "Responsive, too," he said, aware that his voice was thickening. This was torture, but torture of the best kind.

He leaned in, pressing a kiss on her lips, just a light one because there was another place he wanted to kiss more. Lowering his head, he took her nipple into his mouth, sucking gently at first, then more strongly. When she grabbed his shoulders for support, he knew a very real sense of male triumph.

Abby was his, for tonight at least, and she was filling other holes inside him, empty places left by the winds of fame, the ugliness of divorce and the battle for his daughter. Yes, they'd find forgetfulness tonight, but even as the yearning swamped him, he hoped there'd be more than that.

She shivered as he sucked her nipple, then her fingers dug into him as he withdrew his mouth and moved to her other breast. As he sucked, he felt as if the rhythm of his pull matched the rhythmic pounding in his loins. With each passing second, his entire body was growing heavier until he felt he could barely stand.

At last he pulled his mouth from her breast, blowing lightly on her damp nipple, listening with delight to the groan that escaped her. Gently he urged her onto the bed and slipped off her jogging pants, underwear and socks. At last she lay naked in front of him, illumined only by the dim light from the bedside lamp and the little bit of light the storm allowed through one tall window. A contrast of cool and hot in the light, outlining her every charm.

And she had plenty of them. She watched almost sleepily as he stripped the rest of his clothes, then knelt naked between her legs. She reached up at once, running her palms over him as if she wanted to touch every inch of him. Her hips began a gentle rocking, a come-hither that called to him as strongly as any siren's sound.

Spreading her legs even wider, he looked down at her most private place, surrounded by a thick brown thatch that barely concealed the warm cleft in the center. Bending, he ran his tongue over her, tasting her sensitive nub. She cried out, but didn't push him away. Instead she tried to pull him closer.

Her hands ran over his chest, then she stunned him by reaching down and grabbing his erection. The sensation electrified him, driving everything else from his mind. He pumped in her hand, not sure how long he'd be able to hang on to his self-control. Long enough to dig a condom out of the bedside table, but no longer. Her hands fumbled with his as she helped roll it on, the sexiest thing ever except for her.

Her eagerness matched his. Slowly, carefully, he lowered himself, taking care as he entered her, aware it had been a while. She gasped, her eyes closing, and her whole body reached up to meet him.

Buried at last deep within her, he kissed her, this time driving his tongue into her mouth, mimicking the movements of his hips until it felt as if they were rocking themselves up a huge pinnacle of need.

He felt explosions throughout his body, nerve endings crackled with excitement, his loins ached with need. Rising on one elbow he put his hand between them and found her sensitive nub of nerves, determined that she come with him.

And come with him she did. Higher and higher until her soft cries seemed to meld with all the pounding sensations inside of him, goading him, satisfying him all at once. Then he heard the cry and heard her stiffen, arching up into him.

With one more thrust he followed her over the top into the glory beyond.

Abby felt as if she'd entered a new universe. Her release had been so strong that it almost hurt. She lay beneath Rory, exhausted, joyful, sated. One thing she knew for sure, Porter had never made her feel like this. His lovemaking had been perfunctory, more about his enjoyment than hers.

Which had made it so much easier to believe the criticisms he had hurled at her.

Rory groaned and lifted his head. "Be right back."

He withdrew from her carefully, then disappeared into his bathroom. A short while later he returned and literally hopped into the bed with her, grinning.

She had to smile back, although she was sure she couldn't move a muscle. The torpor that filled her was delicious, and she didn't want to lose it.

He threw the covers back, and cold air drifted across her heated skin. "You are so beautiful," he said. As if to prove it, he ran his palm over her from her shoulders to her knees, then followed up with a light sprinkling of kisses, before pulling the comforter over them again and drawing her into his arms.

"You're pretty beautiful yourself," she offered, finding it hard to talk.

"Is this the point where I ask if it was as good for me as it was for you?"

As his reversal of words struck her, a laugh escaped her. "Silly."

"Well, it's more entertaining than the right way. Personally, I thought it was fabulous, and if you don't object, I want you again."

Of course she didn't object. The thought that he wanted her again made her toes curl with delight. "It was wonderful. Totally wonderful."

And totally unlike her previous experience. She expected him to roll over and go to sleep the way Porter always had, but instead he continued to lie beside her, gazing at her and smiling. In all the weeks she had known him, she had seldom seen him looking this relaxed.

But to be fair, it had been months since *she* had felt this relaxed.

"I hope," he said, "that you feel as beautiful as you are."

She colored faintly. "Don't embarrass me."

"The truth shouldn't embarrass you. I think you're beautiful. And since I already got what I wanted, I don't need to lie."

She drew a sharp breath, astonished, then giggled and pushed his shoulder lightly. "You'll go to my head."

"There are other places I'd like to go, as well."

She ducked her head into his shoulder, inhaling his wonderful, musky scent and wondered how she could have missed this. With Porter there had been little foreplay, and certainly no afterplay. He'd have been snoozing by now.

Maybe it was time to stop making comparisons. Maybe it was time to just appreciate the moment in hand. Tomorrow would come soon enough.

He tilted his head a little. "It sounds like the wind is dying down. And I guess I should take care of Rally. Do you want to wait for me here or come down with me?"

She wanted to stay in his bed forever, but decided it might be best to carry on as if nothing had changed. Because it probably hadn't, except for the wonderful seeds of warmth he'd planted deep inside her frozen heart.

"I'll come."

Oddly, she felt no embarrassment as she climbed out of bed and put her clothes on, even though Rory made no secret of the pleasure he took in watching her dress. His admiring gaze really *did* make her feel beautiful.

They walked downstairs hand in hand to find the dog waiting patiently beside his empty bowls. He looked as if he'd endured his separation from them out of good manners, but he was running out of patience. It was enough to make her grin.

As soon as Rory headed for the back door, the Great Dane scrambled to his feet and hurried along. While Rory took care of the walk, Abby filled the water bowl. That animal could sure drink.

Beyond the windows, the blowing snow had settled. The day was still steely gray, but the world, far from being buried in white, looked as if it had received only a light dusting of snow. Most of it, she surmised, had blown to places where it could blow no farther, in gullies and up against buildings. And, apparently, across the roads, to judge by what Nancy Nash had said.

She popped over to the small TV over the counter and turned on the weather. More snow to come, a list of roads closed by drifting snow, possibility of school cancellation.

Wow!

Rory and the dog drifted back in just in time to catch the last of the forecast.

"Well, that doesn't sound good. Nancy may get awfully tired of having both girls if this goes on another day."

"I don't know," Abby answered. "When I was that age, my girlfriends and I pretty much were self-entertaining. We'd hide in a bedroom so nobody would bother us."

"Maybe I should call anyway."

He picked up the phone and dialed. Moments later he was clearly being assured by Nancy Nash that the girls weren't any trouble at all. When he hung up, he was smiling.

"Nancy says they're less trouble together than Betsy is on her own."

Abby had no trouble believing that. All of a sudden, she felt a little awkward. Her role as housekeeper no longer fit exactly, but she wasn't sure what other role she had. She turned back to the coffeepot as if it fascinated her.

She heard Rory move, then strong arms encircled her waist and he kissed the nape of her neck. "You love that coffeepot?"

Shivers of desire rippled through her. She leaned back against him, marveling at his strength and the hardness of his muscles. "It's a strong urge, you know," she managed lightly. "When I first saw it I was over-whelmed. Now I figure it's the best coffeepot ever invented. I don't even have to be fully awake to use it."

"My mom used to make it on the stove in a tin pot that must have been a hundred years old. Well, probably not, but it was battered enough. When I discovered drip coffee, I thought I'd died and gone to heaven."

Her laugh came out a bit breathless and ragged. "Yeah."

"You said you used to help in your family's business. What was it?"

"Do you remembered the catalog store over on First?"

"Do I ever." He turned, keeping his arms loosely around her so that they were face-to-face. Her hands settled on his narrow waist. "Trips to the catalog store were among my favorite things. That was your parents'? What happened?"

"The internet and online buying. Good for delivery services, not good for catalog stores."

He nodded, frowning faintly. "I hadn't thought about that, but yeah, I can see it. So they had to shut down?"

"About five years ago. Couldn't meet the bills anymore."

"I'm sorry."

She shrugged. "Times change."

"Unfortunately, sometimes." He released her and went to sit at the table. "Yeah, I remember the catalogs. Mom loved to pore over them. I hadn't really thought about it, but those big old catalogs were a staple of ranch life at one time. Lots of folks called them wishbooks."

"A staple of a lot of lives. Anyway, it kept getting worse, and then they couldn't afford any help, so I worked for them for a few years. After that... well, I think I told you my dad found a job in Colorado Springs."

"Are they doing okay?"

"Dad can't work anymore. Heart condition. He's on disability and Mom works at some big box store for a little extra. Otherwise they're fine."

"How come you didn't go with them?"

She shook her head and turned back to the coffeepot. "They wanted me to go to college. By the time they moved I was old enough to be a resident on my own here, and I could get in-state tuition. They helped as much as they could."

"Then Porter."

"Then Porter." The coffee had finished brewing and she pulled down two mugs. "Coffee cake?"

"The only thing I'm hungry for is you."

Her heart nearly stopped in her breast.

"But I'll give you a break. Coffee cake will be nice. Let me get it out."

They sat together at the table, but she all of a sudden found it hard to meet his gaze. Had he really meant that? Would he have said it if he hadn't? But then Porter had made vows to her that hadn't even survived a whole year, from what she gathered. And why should she need a break? Was he just kindly brushing her off?

Agonizing thoughts ran through her mind and emotions, primary among them: had she just been the world's worst fool?

"Abby?" His hand suddenly rested over hers on the table. "I can feel that shell closing around you again. Did I do something?"

"No," she murmured. How much of her fear came from her imagination? This man hadn't made any promises, but would she have believed them if he had? No, the trouble rested all inside her.

"I find that hard to believe."

Astonished, she finally forgot herself enough to look at him.

"What do you want from me, Abby?"

"I don't…"

"Maybe you do." His voice had taken on an edge.

"Everyone wants something. Why should you be any different?"

His words pierced her like a shaft through her heart. She clearly wasn't the only one with trust issues. Yet this attack seemed to prove out her own doubts. She couldn't trust him. How had she trusted him far enough to let him make love to her?

"Rory, stop."

"Stop what? I made love to you. It was something special, I thought, but now here you are curling up inside yourself again. The things that are running across your face tell me I didn't make you happy. So what's missing, Abby? What do you want from me?"

"How dare you!" In an instant she erupted, shoving back from the table. "I'm not for sale and you can take your damn job and shove it. I quit!"

She stormed out of the kitchen, wondering how the hell she was going to get out of here in the midst of a worsening storm. Well, she could hide out in her apartment until it cleared. Even he couldn't be messed up enough to tell her to leave in a blizzard, and even if he was she didn't have to listen.

She slammed her door and for the first time she locked it.

Only then did fury give way to tears. What had just happened? She'd been wrestling with her own demons and suddenly his had emerged in the most ugly way possible.

Oh, they both had demons, and the less time they spent together, the better.

Burying her face in her pillow, she sobbed her heart out.

No man could be trusted. No man.

Chapter Seven

The storm worsened through the rest of the afternoon. Rory sat at the piano, hammering the keys, wondering what devil had taken hold of him to talk to Abby that way. He played out anger and rage that he seldom gave expression to, while the renewed storm battered the world.

Not enough sleep. Lousy excuse. Twenty years of discovering that his worth largely rested in a talent that was a gift, a lot of hard work and what he could do for other people. He liked doing for other people, but he sure as hell didn't like knowing that's all they wanted him for.

Stella was a case in point. But Abby wasn't like that, damn it. How had that all come surging out of him? The way she had looked, the anguish on her face, and the worst of it was that there was no way to take back angry words. No way at all.

He'd destroyed whatever little trust she'd started to feel for him, and he didn't even know why.

He pounded the keys harder, abusing a beautiful instrument, trying to get to his innermost core. Hell, wasn't that what he'd come out here to do? He was finding, however, that the boy he'd been was gone, replaced by a man he didn't always like.

Right now, he didn't like himself at all. What had gotten into him? A woman who looked worried and frightened? She had every right, given what had happened to her, given who he was and her presumption that sooner or later he'd go back to his old life. A realistic presumption, one he couldn't blame her for.

But that meant she was struggling with herself, struggling with the trust she had offered him in his bed earlier, struggling with the fact that there were no promises, no future, no nothing except some great lovemaking.

Nor were either of them in a position to consider anything else. Damn, he was glad Regina wasn't here. He didn't want her to see this ugly side of him.

So why had he erupted? Other than too little sleep, what about watching Abby pull back into her shell had disturbed him that much? The feeling that his own trust had once again been betrayed? Or the feeling that he hadn't won hers? God, he'd said words to her he hadn't even said to Stella, and she was the one who should have heard them.

He hated himself.

How had he let himself become so cynical? So hideous? So untrusting? And why? Sure there had been a lot of groupies, but those women had understood the rules. Stella had been a different game, actually winning his love before she threw it on the trash heap once she'd gotten the career push she wanted. Maybe he was more like Abby than he'd even realized.

And if that was the case, he sure as hell should have been more understanding.

His fingers froze on the keys. Was he running scared? The question stuttered in his mind then steadied and remained predominant. Was he?

If so, from what?

He wanted to beat his head on something to shake it loose, reorder it, find the basis for his unforgivable attack on Abby. For a fact she'd never trust him now, nor would he deserve it.

He needed his head examined. Somehow something in him had gotten twisted out of all reason. Stella? The loss of his daughter? The looming custody battle? Was he trying to paint everyone with Stella's colors?

Was he afraid?

He didn't like being afraid. Fear wasn't a huge factor in his nature. Little scared him, and he liked it that way. All his life he'd trusted himself to deal with whatever came along. But if it was fear, fear of what? Another Stella? Hell, she couldn't possibly have a clone, and Abby couldn't possibly be anything like her.

Damn, he was messed up.

But now he'd messed up someone else, especially unforgivable since he'd been trying to gain her trust and pry her out of her shell. Then he'd gone and shoved her right back in again.

He couldn't believe himself.

He also knew something else. The longer he let this lie between them, the deeper her hurt would grow. Bad enough that he'd demanded to know what she wanted from him. Worse to let her keep thinking he'd meant to hurt her that way. She'd jumped up and said she wasn't for sale. God, that he'd even implied that...

Unable to stand himself another moment, he went to her room and knocked on the door. No answer. He waited, then knocked louder. "Abby?"

"Go away."

Well, at least she was still breathing. He pressed his forehead to the door, filled with so much self-disgust and anger he wondered if he should even attempt this now. But once again he could almost feel the pain hardening, becoming permanent. He couldn't leave her like this.

"Abby, I need to talk to you."

Suddenly the door flew open and she glared at him from puffy eyes. "I think you talked enough."

"I wasn't even talking to *you*!" The words ripped out of him, torn from a knot of misery that seldom left him anymore.

"I didn't see anyone else in that room." She sounded hoarse, from crying he guessed.

"Oh, there were other people there. Stella for one."

Her chin jutted a bit. "Yeah? Why take it out on me?"

"I shouldn't have," he admitted quietly. "I was wrong. Overtired, on edge from this custody thing... but that's no excuse." Then he said the most humbling words of all. "I was afraid."

Something in her face changed. She didn't answer for what felt like an eternity. "So am I."

"I know, which makes what I did even worse. It

was unforgivable. I am so sorry. I'll leave you alone now."

But as he turned away, he felt her touch his arm tentatively. He squeezed his eyes shut as another wave of anguish poured through him. That she should be tentative in her touch after their lovemaking made his chest feel like it was caving in. God, what had he done?

"Abby?" he said hoarsely, hardly daring to let a splinter of hope enter his private hell.

"Let's talk," she said, her voice choked and tight.

He turned back to her, slowly. "Are you sure?"

"Give me a minute, I just got out of the shower."

So he went to the kitchen, a room that had begun to feel less sterile as they had filled it with memories of the three of them having dinner together, with Regina's happy chatter. With some kind of misbegotten hope where there probably was none.

The coffee had turned bitter, so he made a fresh pot. They hadn't eaten since breakfast, not even the Danish he had put out just before the blowup. He tested it with a finger and decided it hadn't gone stale. Then he waited.

She appeared finally, clad in lemon-yellow sweats and socks. Her hair was still damp, and pulled back into a pony tail. She sat across from him after getting some coffee.

He regarded her from eyes that seemed to burn, that felt heavy with unshed emotions. Hollow. He felt almost hollowed out except for the river of pain and frustration that filled his every corner. He was caught in a web of his own making, with no way to get out.

From Regina, to Stella, to his career, to Abby, he felt wrapped in wires of steel he couldn't break.

"You need some sleep," she finally said.

"Yeah. Only I'm not gonna get it. I just smashed something that I never wanted to smash."

"I've heard worse."

He felt like erupting all over again. Closing his hands so tightly around his mug, he was surprised it didn't shatter, he answered, "I know. Damn it, I know. That's what makes me lower than a slug. You didn't deserve that."

"Neither of us deserves a lot of things. The same could be said about most people." She sighed. "You hurt me and I'm not going to pretend you didn't. But given the last couple of days..."

"Oh, I'm not taking that excuse. I don't deserve it."

She looked down and didn't answer for a minute. When she raised her gaze, she met his directly. "I was thinking, once I'd calmed down, that past relationships cloud new ones."

"How so?"

"I was sitting here thinking about Porter, about my own crippling fears—and I'll be honest, Rory, they'd been crippling me for a while—and struggling against them when you...blew up. None of what you were seeing on my face had anything to do with you."

He cussed quietly. "Big misread."

"And then you retorted. Maybe not because of anything I'd done, but because of things you were used to from the past. We all carry those hot buttons with us."

"I already told you I was reacting to Stella and... other things."

"Exactly."

He ran his fingers through his hair and jumped up. "Well, doesn't that create one hopeful future."

"Maybe it does once you recognize what's going on." She rose, too. "You must need dinner."

"You quit," he reminded her.

"I just got rehired. But quitting gave me so much satisfaction."

He almost gaped at her, and then a weary chuckle escaped him. "You are one amazing woman, Abby Jason."

"You make a fan club of one."

"No." He reached for her, taking her by the shoulders. "Don't keep telling yourself that lie. You're remarkable in so many ways, even if you can't see it." Then, realizing he'd touched her without permission, he quickly dropped his hands. "Dinner can wait. Please. The kind of empty I'm running on won't be filled by food."

She hesitated, then resumed her seat. "At least eat some Danish."

He grabbed a thick piece and put it on one of the dessert plates that had been waiting since hours ago. He eschewed the fork and simply took a big bite before setting it down. "Okay?"

"Better." She took a much smaller piece for herself. "I don't want Regina to come back to this tension. We have some work to do."

Thinking about his daughter in the midst of all this? His heart cracked a little, and he felt touched beyond words. Remarkable didn't even begin to cut it with Abby. Stella wouldn't have given a darn. "Maybe

I've been hanging around with the wrong people," he remarked.

"I know I was, obviously." She glanced toward the darkening window. "I could almost swear this storm is getting worse."

"Maybe. The one inside the house is getting a little better, I hope."

Her gaze trailed back to him. "Maybe. I guess we get to spend some time being our own therapists."

"How do you want to do that?"

"By parsing out exactly what is goading us. What we're afraid of, what hurt us, what's worrying us. We don't have to do it together. We can go to separate corners and make private lists if you want."

God, he wanted to hug her. "I think it might do us both good to know what devils the other one is dealing with. You've told me about Porter, I've told you a little about Stella, but that doesn't exactly cover the hot buttons they left behind. Not all of them."

"I guess not." She nibbled at her Danish while he finished his and took another slab.

"We can't just go back to being employer and employee," he remarked. "Not after today. We crossed some lines...and I don't regret it. But now, I guess now we need to find a way to be friends."

"That requires trust," she said quietly. "I don't think either of us is feeling a whole lot of that."

He couldn't deny it, but his stomach sank as he accepted the truth of it. Two distrusting souls might find the whole friendship thing beyond reach. Was he going to allow that? But how could he change it?

He'd been trying and had blown it all to hell. How

could he be sure he wouldn't do it again? Equally, how could *she* be sure he wouldn't lash out again?

The problem appeared insurmountable.

Rory finally dozed off on the living room couch. For some reason he didn't want to go to bed, although Abby could sort of understand that, given that only a few hours ago they'd made love there. Maybe she should go change out the sheets, remove the memories and scents of the time they had spent there.

Erase herself from his bedroom.

For some reason, that made her spine stiffen. No way. If he was having regrets about it now, he could change his own darn sheets.

The night was deepening, though it was not yet late. Wind still howled, creating the unusual possibility that school might be cancelled tomorrow. She figured she could count on both hands the number of times that had happened in her life here. Sometimes ranch kids missed school, but actually shutting down? Almost never.

She wondered if she was going to sit there all night watching Rory sleep, or staring at the laptop screen that had long since decided to take its own nap. She could go to her room and do something, but for some reason she couldn't make herself do it.

What had happened earlier had been ugly, but she could understand it. He was reacting to Stella. She'd been sitting there thinking about Porter. Were the two of them to be forever imprisoned in dead relationships?

And Rory had additional concerns. She had watched the anger and frustration when he realized Stella was making false claims to regain custody of Regina, and if there was one thing she knew for certain now, it was that Rory loved his daughter. Truly loved her. Clearly this was a man who, once he'd given his heart, didn't take it back easily. Stella had thrown him away, just as Porter had thrown her away.

Maybe she should be more understanding.

No, she wasn't going to endure another attack like that. He clearly regretted it, but she wasn't going to become a stand-in for Stella. She had enough on her own plate to deal with.

But she could still understand. The last couple of days had been incredibly hard for him.

She dozed off, too, finally, really relaxing for the first time in hours. Sleep carried her to a place where she found herself in a beautiful gown staring at her reflection in the mirror. "See?" said a voice. "You're beautiful."

She awakened reluctantly to a bump on her knee and looked around the computer to see the dog. Time for walking and feeding. Probably well past.

She set the computer on the side table and rose. His tail wagged a couple of times and he gave her a grin. Really fickle, she thought with amusement.

She stepped out back with him into the storm and realized it was indeed getting worse. Colder, too. Even inside her jacket, she felt chilled.

Rally wasted no time and darted back inside with evident relief. In the kitchen she filled his bowl as she had seen Regina and Rory do so many times, and replaced his water. Missing Regina hadn't killed the dog's appetite at all.

She heard a light step and turned to see Rory standing just inside the kitchen, stretching until she heard pops. "Ah, that felt good," he remarked and headed for the coffee.

"It's probably stale."

"I've had worse. Did you get any sleep?"

"I dozed some."

"Good. Feeling any better?"

She didn't know exactly how to answer that. She'd forgiven his outburst, but forgiving wasn't the same as forgetting.

"I'll leave you alone," he said quietly and returned to the living room with his coffee.

She stood with the dog in the kitchen and realized this couldn't continue. She'd go nuts from the strain if he was always avoiding her, and honestly, she didn't want to avoid him. He'd apologized. She'd be more careful. If he did it again, that would be it. But in the meantime…

She headed back to the living room. His guitar stood propped against the couch, near where he sat. She took her usual chair and waited. For what she didn't exactly know.

He was leaning back, legs loosely crossed, hands folded on his flat belly, eyes closed. After a moment they opened. "Are you afraid of me?" he asked bluntly.

She thought about it, wanting to be completely honest. "Cautious, not afraid."

"Fair enough. But I've never lied to you, Abby. Not once. You've seen me angry, ugly, furious, despairing and ready to go to war. That's the real, unexpurgated me. I can be volatile. I'm not always calm and measured. And today…I lost my common sense, as well. You're not Stella. You couldn't be Stella if you tried. If you've got a mean bone in your body, it still wouldn't add up to all the mean bones in Stella's. I should never have unleashed my anger with her at you."

"No," she agreed. "But we already talked about this. I'm beginning to think we're both full of mine-fields."

"Hot buttons, you said. I fear you may be right. I'd like to work on getting past them somehow. I happen to like you."

That warmed her a little. Unfortunately, she suspected she'd gone past liking with him. At least until that scene earlier. Now she felt confused and concerned. How did anyone get over all the scars life had left behind? She hadn't a clue.

"Well, I'm going to start practicing gut checks."

"What?"

He shrugged. "Halt my tongue and reaction for a moment and ask myself what I'm really reacting to."

"You can do that?"

"Yeah. And unless I'm half out of my mind with lack of sleep and worry, it usually works. It has to, or I'd have offended my way out of a job."

She pondered that for a few minutes. It sounded like a good idea, and she wondered if she'd be able to do it. Oh, keeping her mouth shut had become a habit since Porter, but keeping her emotions in check? How often had she retreated into a private maelstrom of feelings and spent time arguing with herself? Apparently it didn't help much.

"You said," she began cautiously, "that people always want something from you."

"Invariably, except for a few good friends. A lot of people see me as the road to something they want. It's not surprising. When you've been blessed the way I have, other people would like to share a little of that. As long as they're honest, I don't mind."

"But they're not always honest?"

"The world is full of sycophants. They think if they stroke my ego enough, I'll be so flattered I'll do something for them. Pay their gambling debts, get them a recording contract, hire them as an opening act. Whole loads of things. And I get it. I just don't like it when they're not up-front about it."

She nodded, understanding insofar as she could. "But you help a lot of people?"

"The ones I can. People helped me, after all."

"And some profited from you."

"That's all part of it, isn't it." He sat up, unfolding his legs and resting his elbows on his knees. "There's one big difference between us, Abby. I know people want things from me. You don't believe anyone does or could want anything from you."

The words hit home hard. She faced the stark reality of just how much Porter had really gutted her. He'd killed her sense of self-worth so completely that she'd even avoided her girlfriends until just recently. Feeling like a drag, feeling like she had nothing to offer. Feeling that she was an object of pity and scorn.

Was any of that even true?

"Well," he said when she remained silent, "we can't solve this overnight. Just know that I wanted to spend the day making love with you, and instead I acted like an ass. Because of my own problems, not you. I can't fix it. I just hope you can forgive me. And I don't want to lose you. Yeah, I could get another housekeeper, but Regina would be upset, and frankly so would I. I like sharing this house with you. She just plain likes you, and whether or not you know it, you're a good role model for her."

She felt flattered, but was still struggling to believe the nice things he said about her. The walls between them, she realized, were largely of her own building, and she didn't quite know what to do about it.

"I'm going up to bed," he said, rising.

"But you haven't had dinner."

"I couldn't eat to save my life. I'm wallowing in self-disgust here. Just let me."

All alone once again, she looked down the tunnel of her past and into the empty tunnel of her future.

Was she going to try to break down those walls? Could she take the risk? Could she try to build something more positive?

The wind howled but didn't answer.

Much later, after giving the dog a fresh bowl of water and a walk, she found herself climbing the stairs rather than going to her own apartment. She was facing her demons, she realized, and in a way that could buy her a lot of trouble. After this evening, maybe she deserved rejection, but she wasn't sure she could survive it.

She had something to prove to herself, that Porter hadn't broken her forever. That she could reach for what she wanted, despite the way he had trashed her. Going for it had become imperative.

She wanted Rory. He'd said he wanted her, too. If he was lying about it, she'd know for sure whether she was attractive to him. A rejection would probably send her to a convent or something, but she had to know. This issue needed to be settled. To hell with tomorrow, and long-term. She needed to know that she was indeed an attractive woman. That earlier hadn't been a fluke. That now that he'd made love to her he wouldn't be glad to forget her.

The need to know terrified her and drove her all at the same time. She never would have imagined how much courage it took to climb those stairs as frightened as she was. But somewhere deep inside, she needed knowledge, and with any luck she'd never be afraid to reach out again.

The dog came with her. She grabbed his scruff briefly for courage, then felt him lick her hand as if to tell her she wasn't alone.

Rory's bedroom door stood open, surprising her, but all was dark within. Rally's nails clicked a little on the wood floor and when they reached the door, she stopped. Rally didn't.

"Need a walk, boy?" she heard Rory ask sleepily. "I just walked him."

Silence. Then a rustle of bedding and a click as he turned on a lamp. "Abby? Is something wrong?"

"I don't know." Stupid answer. Anxiety was ripping through her, threatening to glue her tongue to the roof of her mouth. "Is it all right to want *you*?"

He didn't move immediately, suspending her somewhere between heaven and hell. Then he reached for the corner of the bedding and pulled back the sheet and comforter. She could see his bare chest, and the waistband of his flannel pants. "It's okay. Climb in," he said quietly.

So she did, trembling from head to foot, her heart racing uncomfortably. She didn't know what to do, what to say, but he asked nothing of her. She still wore her shirt and pants, which she'd have slept in, this cold night, and as she lay with her back to him, he pulled the covers over her.

He surprised her by rolling onto his side and wrapping one arm around her. "Sleep," he murmured. "You've got to be exhausted."

In his arms, surrounded by him, her fears evaporated and she stopped trembling. She felt inexplicably safe and sleep became the easiest thing in the world.

During the night, something changed. Abby popped her eyes open and saw the digital clock by the bed. Nearly 5:00 a.m. She felt a warm whisper on her neck and realized it must be Rory's breath. She closed her eyes again, wishing she could stay like this forever.

"Awake?" he murmured.

"Just."

"Mmm." His arm tightened around her waist and tugged her closer until she could feel his erection pressed to her bottom. "Ignore me," he mumbled. "Can't help what you do to me."

In that instant she felt as if her heart had taken wing. Wearing her sweats, she could do that to him? Maybe she wasn't such a cow after all.

"You feel so good," he whispered.

Oh, yeah, she did. Better than the first time she'd lain in his arms.

"You feel good, too," she whispered back.

He continued to hold her, making no moves of

any kind. After a bit, she thought he'd fallen back to sleep and gradually drowsiness overcame her again. The last two days had been hard, and neither of them had gotten anywhere near enough sleep. Secure and warm, she drifted away again.

Morning dawned with blinding sunlight. Abby woke as it struck her eyelids and she blinked, feeling as if she had forgotten what a bright day looked like.

Rory still held her, but almost as soon as she recognized it, the phone rang.

He groaned and rolled over, reaching for the set beside the bed. "Hi. Yeah, just woke. Okay. I love you, too."

"Regina?" she asked, her voice still thick with sleep.

"Yup. School's closed but Nancy's bringing her home in an hour or so. Time to face the day."

Abby immediately sat up, a kind of panic setting in. "I need to clean up, change sheets…"

Rory chuckled quietly and pulled her back down, cupping her face between his hands. "In a minute," he said, his face still soft from sleep. "First, though…" He kissed her, kissed her more deeply than he had before, his tongue tasting the inside of her mouth, immediately stoking the fire within her.

"Rory…" she gasped his name when he finally lifted his head.

"I know. I'll change the bed. You go take a nice long shower." He continued to cup her face, however, studying her. "Are we square?"

"Square enough." Although she wasn't quite sure what she meant by that. A lot of the tension had left her when she'd climbed into his bed last night and been welcomed so easily. Welcomed chastely. Why that meant so much to her she'd have to puzzle out later. Right now she had to put things to rights so Regina wouldn't be wondering what the two of them had been up to. There was nothing in what had happened that should trouble that girl in the least.

And there probably never would be.

She quickly drew his face down to give him a quick kiss, letting him know that for now it was all okay. She couldn't look beyond that. Not yet.

After a shower, she found Rory had already put his sheets in the laundry and replaced them with a fresh set. Before long, the two of them were eating a light breakfast of English muffins and eggs while they waited for Regina.

She could feel the impatience in Rory. He'd missed his daughter.

"Was there a reason she's coming home?" Abby asked. "Didn't Nancy say she'd keep the girls if school was closed?"

"No, if the roads were bad. The woman's had those two girls on her hands since Friday afternoon. Can you blame her for wanting to get back to normal?"

"Actually, no."

He smiled crookedly. "I'll be glad to get back to normal, too. Having her back again has reminded me how much I'd been missing her."

He rose to get himself more coffee and dropped a kiss on her head as he passed. A silly smile came to her face. How fast things could change.

When Regina returned, Abby remained in the kitchen like a good housekeeper. She heard Rory talking to Nancy and couldn't mistake Rally's joy. It was so overwhelming he ran round and round the house while Regina laughed.

Regina popped into the kitchen. "Hey, Abby."

"Hey, yourself. You've been missed."

Regina looked down at the grinning dog. "I can tell. He nearly knocked me over when I came in the house and he's been running all over the place."

"I heard. Can I get you something?"

Regina shook her head. "I'm not hungry this morning."

Abby felt a spark of concern. "Are you sick?"

"I think I ate too much this weekend. Chips, soda, popcorn, chocolate." She stuck her tongue out a bit. "I'm overdone. Come on, Rally, let's go out back."

Abby heard Nancy leave, and a moment later Rory joined her. "Where's Regina?"

"Out back running Rally. Or maybe running herself. She said she ate too much over the weekend."

He nodded, but no smile lit his face.

"Rory?"

"Nancy said she thought Regina was acting a little off this morning. Maybe coming down with some kind of bug. That's why she brought her back so early."

Again she felt that flicker of concern. "Well, how bad can it be if she's out running the dog?"

"Yeah." He summoned a smile. "I worry too much."

She didn't think so, but she didn't tell him that. It seemed odd to her that a girl that age would be talking about having eaten too much food. It might be why she thought she was a little under the weather but at her age not very likely.

She heard the back door open, heard the dog run happily down the hall, and a cold blast of air preceded Regina. She popped in, looking rosy from the cold and pulled out a chair to join them at the table.

"Miss me?" she asked.

"Like the dickens," Rory answered, smiling.

"Very much," Abby said truthfully.

"I missed you guys, too. So, Dad, about that horse…"

Rory rolled his eyes and Regina giggled. "No horse, not right now. But keep bugging me. You never know when you may win."

Abby spoke lightly. "You could ride Rally."

Hearing his name, the dog gave a rare *woof* and wagged his tail mightily. Clearly everything was right in his universe again.

Regina laughed then turned to her father. "Dad?"

"I think that's me."

The girl grinned at him. "So Betsy's family is getting ready to decorate for Christmas. They were getting the boxes out while I was there. Do we have any decorations?"

Rory looked flummoxed. "Uh…"

"I didn't think so. So Abby can take me shopping right after Thanksgiving? I want to decorate."

"If it's okay by Abby…"

"No problem," she answered. "I'd enjoy that." In fact, the idea really appealed to her.

"Okay then. You gals do up the house. But there's one thing I insist on."

Regina scowled. "What?"

"That when it's time to get the tree I'm going along, too."

Regina squealed and threw herself at him for a huge hug. "You're the best. And Dad?"

I think I already identified myself."

Regina giggled. "No, it's something else. I wrote my first song."

He sat up a little straighter. "Really? What brought that on?"

"Well, I kind of always wanted to. It's like there's this music running in my head a lot of the time."

He smiled and reached for his daughter's hand. "I know all about that. Can I hear it?"

"Not yet. I'm not completely happy with the words." She turned to Abby. "I want you to help me with them."

"Me?" Abby was startled. "I don't know anything about music."

"But you're good with words. You helped me with my English paper. And you mentioned you liked to write. So…"

"But your dad writes lyrics all the time."

"This is a Christmas present for him," Regina said, rolling her own eyes and looking so much like Rory for an instant that it was almost like having double vision.

"Do I need to head for the barn?" Rory asked. "Am I cast out for a while?"

A short while later, Regina did indeed banish him.

"I was thinking about this over the weekend after my mother called," Regina explained to Abby once Rory disappeared toward his barn studio. "Nobody does anything for him. Nobody makes him feel truly loved."

"You do," Abby said gently, her heart aching.

"That's a kid thing. Of course I love my dad. But I want to give him something special, just for him. Something I didn't buy in a store. Something special just from me."

"I get the feeling that just being you is special enough for him, but I understand what you're saying. I don't know how much help I'll be, though."

"You can help me polish."

"I'll try."

The sentiments in Regina's lyrics were trite and juvenile. Of course they were. But as Rory had said, things became trite because they touched people. Plus, Regina was only ten. Mainly she needed help with meter and word choice to finish it off, a darling little poem about how a girl is always carried in her father's heart, and there's no safer place to be. Abby offered only minimal suggestions, because this was Regina's gift to her father and she wanted that to shine through.

But when Regina sat down at the piano to play the melody she'd created for the words, it all changed. A beautiful, brief, but haunting piece that touched Abby to her core. The girl was a born musician and she had a voice as pure as a flute.

"That's beautiful." They both started as Rory spoke. "Don't let me interrupt," he said, his eyes shining suspiciously. "But that's really beautiful, Regina."

"You weren't supposed to hear it yet," she said, but she beamed from ear to ear. "Merry Christmas, Daddy. Early."

Rory looked at Abby. "You ever sing?"

"Alto for a while in the church choir. That's it."

"Then how about we go out to the studio and record Regina's song? Abby can harmonize on the chorus. Later if you want we can add more instrumentation."

"But…" Abby's protests were lost as Regina jumped up excitedly. She didn't know the first thing about singing a background vocal, in fact very little about singing at all, but somehow her protests got drowned and she was dragged by the two of them out to the barn.

The studio was even more impressive than she recalled from her one brief viewing. She couldn't imagine how much all the equipment had cost, not to mention the keyboards, drums and guitars. Equalizers. Recording equipment, microphones…she didn't even know what it all was.

Only after receiving the promise from Rory that her entire vocal track could be erased if it ruined Regina's song did Abby agree to put on headphones and stand at one of the microphones.

Regina started at the keyboard, humming her way through one time. Abby hummed along as requested on the chorus, trying to find the harmony by instinct. Finally she got it, and Rory said, "Let's go. Remember, ladies, it can all be erased if you're not happy."

This was, Abby realized, the happiest father and daughter had looked yet. She supposed it was worth croaking her way through this to make them happy. She had no doubt that Regina's gift had touched Rory as much as she had wanted it to.

The song almost sounded Celtic to Abby, though she couldn't have explained why. Regina's pure soprano filled her ears through the verse and then came her turn at the chorus. Rory pointed at her from the control room, telling her exactly when to join in.

In Daddy's heart love endures
And there I am secure.
Daddy's heart, Daddy's heart,

The place a child should be.
Daddy's heart, Daddy's heart,
The home where I am me.

Regina was all excited when they finished and couldn't wait to hear the playback. Rory obliged, his eyes looking damp. He hugged her first, though, telling him that nobody had ever given him anything as special as that song.

Abby wondered if she should slip back to the house, but before she could take a step in that direction, Regina had drawn her into the hug with Rory.

Then the girl became an impatient ten-year-old again. "Play it again, Dad, please. I can't really hear it right when I sing it."

"No, you can't," Rory agreed. He took them into the control booth, adjusted some buttons and soon the song was emanating from the speakers around them.

Regina's voice was every bit as beautiful as Abby had expected, but her own surprised her. She didn't sound at all like a frog. Not half-bad, she decided. But darned if she was ever going to do that again. She had enough to make her nervous.

Regina turned to her when the song ended. "See, you didn't ruin it at all. You made it better." Then she turned toward Rory, looking suddenly tentative. "Do you like it, Dad?"

He picked her up right off her feet and whirled her around in his arms. "I love it. It's the most beautiful gift ever. And you've got some talent, girl."

"I got it from you," Regina chortled. "If Mom ever wrote a song, it got flushed." Then she giggled.

Abby noted that Rory didn't join in the criticism,

although it might have been tempting. She gave him his due for refusing to denigrate Stella in front of her daughter. Too bad that was a one-way street.

Rory cut three CDs for them, all the while talking to Regina about music. "So you really have it running in your head all the time?"

"Most of the time," Regina said, still happy and beaming. "It stops sometimes when I have to concentrate on schoolwork, but the minute I'm done, it starts coming in snatches again. Just little pieces. This is my first whole song." Then she paused. "I'm not so good with the words, though."

"You did just fine. And that'll come." Rory looked at his daughter, his eyes gleaming with huge pride. "I'm so glad you have the music. Feel free to come in here any time. Or, if you want a guitar..." He looked over to where his "baby" stood propped against a stand. "Maybe it's time you had my grandpa's guitar."

Abby's throat tightened, and she slipped out of the control booth, leaving father and daughter to enjoy their moment of discovery. She knew how much that guitar meant to Rory, yet he was ready to give it to Regina. There was so much love between them.

Back in the house, feeling curiously sad, as if she had glimpsed something beautiful that could never be hers, Abby glanced at the clock and decided to make a special dinner for Regina. Homemade pizza, dough from scratch. With the bread machine to do the kneading and rising, there was time, and she had plenty of marinara sauce left.

She pulled out the machine and started the dough quickly enough. A journey to the pantry found plenty of toppings, although she decided she'd better ask Regina how she felt about things like mushrooms and onions on her pizza. The machine would also be good for making rolls for Thanksgiving and Christmas. Maybe she ought to try that out in the morning. Homesick for something you couldn't quite remember. That was the feeling she had, although she was quite sure she knew what it was. Seeing the magic circle surrounding Rory and his daughter, she had wished she could be part of that kind of love. A vain wish, and she tried to banish it as she sat at the kitchen table with coffee and listened to the bread machine grind and pound away. It was loud, pretty much blocking everything else out.

No time to get maudlin, she warned herself. Something special had happened for Rory and Regina, and she should be cheering it, not bemoaning the fact that her own life was empty of it. Someday, maybe, she'd find that for herself. But in the meantime, she had some demons to deal with and plans to make. The incident with Rory yesterday had made her aware of their hot buttons. Both of them were strewn with them. Best to just keep away from dangerous ground.

A half hour later, Regina returned, Rally at her heels. "Dad has some work to do. He said he'd be back in an hour or so."

Abby almost smiled. She figured Rory would quickly lose track of time and might even forget dinner without Regina to remind him.

"What are you making?" Regina asked as she got a soda, then joined Abby at the table.

"That racket is the bread maker. I'm making pizza dough."

Regina's eyes widened. "Homemade pizza? From scratch? With real dough, not that cracker stuff?"

"Real yeast dough," Abby agreed. "You need to tell me what you want on it."

"I want to help make it!"

"Then you can. All help is welcome." She studied Regina closely, though. The girl's eyes seemed a little shiny. "You feeling okay?"

"I'm fine. Just a tiny bit queasy, but the soda will take care of that. It always does. At least one of my nannies got something right."

Abby had to smile. "Awful nannies? What was the story with them? You don't seem like a whole lot of trouble to me."

"I suppose Mom made it sound worse that it was." Regina rolled her eyes. "Some of them didn't like me. I wasn't always good."

"Who is?"

Regina giggled. "True. The last one, though…all she wanted me to do was stay out of the way so she could have her boyfriend over. I got tired of having to stay in my room any time I wasn't at school or at dance class or soccer practice." She paused. "I was signed up for every activity available. I liked soccer, dancing not so much."

"Piano?"

"Yup, had lessons for that, too."

Abby nodded. "Lots of opportunity."

"Lots of running around. I had fun with most of it, but if I didn't like something, I wasn't allowed to quit." Regina scowled. "I could understand that if I'd insisted I wanted ballet lessons, but I never asked for them and I didn't like them."

Abby nodded sympathetically but said nothing, even though she was getting a picture of an abandoned child.

"It wasn't so bad when my dad was still with us. He insisted I needed free time. Of course, then he'd have to go on tour and I needed to be kept busy again. But he came home a lot to see me." She looked down. "I guess he spent a lot of flying time just to run home and spend a couple days with me between shows. I didn't think about that before." She lifted her head. "He's a good dad. I hope he really likes that song."

"I have absolutely no doubt he loves it. He doesn't strike me as someone who gets tears in his eyes easily."

"No, I never saw him cry." Regina sighed and sipped more coke. "I know I was lucky. Lots of kids wish they could be me."

"But if you could have your way?"

"I'd spend all my time here with Dad. Guess that's not going to happen. Sooner or later he'll have to go back to work." But then she brightened. "But I'll have *you*."

Abby almost panicked. She was quite sure this wasn't what Rory wanted, but she didn't know how to stem Regina's attachment to her. She guessed she was going to have to tell Rory about it soon, before it grew deeper.

"Did I say the wrong thing?" Regina asked. "I mean, if you don't want me around…"

If Abby could have fled right then, she would have. This was going places she had no right to go. She was only the housekeeper and her job might end the instant Rory decided to go back to Nashville. But she couldn't hurt Regina. It just wasn't in her. "I do want you around," she answered. "But keep in mind, I'm just the housekeeper. You dad may have other plans."

"Yeah." Regina tilted her head. "He might. And I might change them." All of a sudden she looked devilish. "How long on that dough?"

The next few hours passed quickly enough. Regina finished her homework then they dug out the pizza pans and Abby taught Regina how to work with the dough.

"I never get to cook," Regina remarked. "Oh, I can make a sandwich or heat a snack in the microwave, but stuff like this? I want you to teach me, Abby. This is cool."

Very cool, Abby thought with a secret smile as flour went everywhere and dough stuck to the counter. Soon enough they had the dough on two pans and then came the toppings.

"Spread the sauce thin," Abby warned her. "You don't want pizza soup."

Regina's concentration was intense as she began to spread the shredded mozzarella and other items. Her tastes weren't limited, and soon they had spread enough pepperoni and vegetables on top of the pizzas to make a thoroughly satisfying meal.

"I think you'll have cold pizza for lunch tomorrow," Abby remarked as they regarded the finished product.

"That's when it's best. I really like it for breakfast." Regina gave her a huge smile. "Thanks for letting me help, Abby."

"You did most of the work."

"I like it. It was fun. So you'll teach me other stuff?"

"Of course." How could she say no to that?

"When do we put them in the oven?"

"As soon as it finishes heating."

"I'll be right back." Regina gathered up her books and papers and stuffed them into her backpack. Moments later she could be heard running up the stairs.

Abby turned to start cleaning the counters, then paused. This was part of cooking, too. Maybe Regina could glean a few lessons about dealing with sticky dough and dry flour.

"Look at that!" Rory said appreciatively. She hadn't heard him come in. "Homemade pizza?"

"Regina did most of the work."

"Most of the mess, too," he guessed, his eyes twinkling. Rally slipped past him and went to work on his water bowl. "Want me to clean up?"

"First, that's my job. Second, I was thinking that if Regina wants to learn to cook, she needs to learn this part, too."

"Good point." He headed straight for the coffee, stepping around some of the flour that dusted the floor. "That song she made for me is beautiful." He sat in the chair Regina had recently vacated.

"Yes, it was," Abby agreed wholeheartedly. "She's talented. Like you."

"She's got a gift, but it's her own. I can't get over that melody."

Abby joined him at the table, much as it went against her grain to leave a mess untouched. "I don't know why, but it sounded a bit Celtic to me."

"It did," he agreed. "Chord progression. It could be played on pipes, too. Amazing from someone her age."

"Be sure to tell Regina that."

He smiled. "I did, repeatedly." Then his smile faded. "I want music to bring her joy. I'm not so sure I want her to follow in my footsteps. Not that it's my decision."

"Relax," said Abby wryly. "We'll probably be back to horses before morning."

She enjoyed watching him laugh. She wondered if Regina knew the demons he'd been dealing with since Stella's call on Saturday, if that had impelled this gift from her. She sure hoped the girl really knew how happy she had made her father.

Regina surprised her by being as eager to learn how to clean up as she had been to cook. She took the warnings about not getting the dry flour wet to heart and repeatedly vacuumed up the dust with a hand vac before they moved on to the stuck dough. A spatula scraped most of it into the sink, then Abby showed her how to use salt as an abrasive to get the rest. That seemed to tickle Regina.

They finished just as the pizzas were ready to come out of the oven. Cooked as perfectly as they could be without a real pizza oven, they sat cooling and bubbling, filling the room with fantastic aromas.

Regina kept inhaling them. "No pizza out of a box ever smelled like that."

Rory spoke. "No pizza out of a box ever tasted like that."

She cocked an eye at him. "How would you know?"

"The nose knows."

More giggling. Abby watched them, smiling, feeling even more envious than before. Even though they included her as part of their circle, she knew deep down that she wasn't and never would be.

"Say," said Rory, while they waited for the pizza to be cool enough to cut, "that song of yours, Regina? It shook something loose for me. I've been trying to get an idea, and you gave me one."

"Great!" Regina put her chin in her hand. "Do I get to hear it?"

"After dinner."

The trouble began a few minutes later. Regina took one bite of her slice, then put it down. Rory was chewing happily, complimenting them both between bites. Abby got halfway through her slice before Regina finally spoke.

"I can't believe I'm not hungry."

The two adults snapped their attention to her. "What's wrong?" they said at the same moment.

"I just feel queasy again. No biggie. But I think I'll go take a nap, if that's okay. Save my pizza."

"Not enough sleep?" Rory asked lightly, but Abby noted how he reached across the table to put his hand on Regina's forehead. "Not feverish," he said with relief. "Actually, you feel cool."

"I'll be okay, Dad," Regina said with a touch of impatience. "I've had an upset stomach before. I think I just need to lie down for a little while."

"Need any help?" he asked.

Now she rolled her eyes. "I'm sure I can get myself into bed."

Silence reigned for a few minutes after she went upstairs. Rory sighed finally and resumed eating.

"Just an upset stomach. A little bug. No point in making more out of it."

"No," Abby agreed quietly. "These things happen. All the excitement, too little sleep and moving to a new place that has a whole crop of germs she's never met before."

He nodded. "I forgot about that. A doctor told me a long time ago that if you move a big distance, you're more likely to get sick for that reason. New bugs. At least that was how he explained why I got so sick sometimes on tour. That and stress."

"I'm sure there are a bazillion bugs I've never met."

He laughed quietly. "I hope we never meet them."

"Do you get sick less often now?"

"On tour? Yeah. I think I met a lot of those bugs the first few years."

"And maybe you don't stress as much. It's all familiar."

A faint frown settled over his face. "Actually, recently it's begun to stress me more. I don't get high on it the way I used to. Weird."

She didn't think it was weird at all. From things he said, she guessed he was a man weary of traveling and working all the time. Weary of constant demands. Like anyone else, he needed time away. Perfectly understandable. That didn't mean he wouldn't change his mind in six months.

Which reminded her of another concern. She hesitated, hating to add anything to his already full plate, but putting it off might compound the problem. If it was a problem.

"Rory? I think Regina's getting too attached to me."

His head lifted. "Too attached?" Then he frowned. "Do you want her to leave you alone?" He clearly didn't really like that.

"No. No! Not at all."

"Then what?" He looked like a man ready to fight, and she shifted uneasily.

"I like Regina bunches. I love having her around. That's not the problem. But she said something…"

"Go on," he pressed, his voice level.

"She said if you went back to touring she could stay here with me."

"And you're not a nanny."

"I didn't say that." Were they going to have another fight? "I didn't know what to say to her because I'm not in control of this situation. I can't make promises. What if you decide you don't need me in six months? That's what worries me. That she'll get attached to me, you'll move on and she won't want to leave me behind and then what? You're stuck with me for the next eight years?"

His expression changed ever so slightly, but the anger was gone. Quietly he said, "I wouldn't call it being stuck with you."

"I just don't want her to get hurt. So I reminded her I'm just the housekeeper, and things could change."

Surprisingly, one corner of his mouth lifted. "To which she answered?"

"That she could change your mind."

A laugh burst out of him then. "Little minx. She probably could. But that doesn't take into account your wishes. I guess I need to speak to her. You want to go to college eventually. Kind of hard to do that and stay here watching her."

Well, that was a message writ large enough to read. Whether he wanted her around or not, he expected her to leave eventually. Two-way street there, she thought, not for the first time.

She tried not to let gloom settle over her. After all, nothing was fixed, nothing was set. Things would change, they always did. But she was a little surprised to realize that leaving Rory and Regina was only going to get harder, and when she thought about it right now, it seemed hard enough. Maybe she should be smart and bail right away.

But that idea nearly killed her. She couldn't just pack up in the morning and walk away. She'd cried her eyes out already after she quit this job. And she remembered the great happiness she had felt being asked to aid Regina with her song, being asked to teach her to cook. Mostly she remembered spending last night chastely in Rory's arms and feeling safe.

How could he do that, make her feel so safe? She'd only seen him here, in this environment. For all she knew he could be a real-life heartbreaker despite what he said about his epiphany. But then she thought of how he cared about his daughter, and she believed he would always do what was best for Regina.

She could trust that in him. Maybe she could trust him even further. But how could she be sure? Porter had lied to her for a long time. Of course, Rory had no reason to lie to her. She was just the hired help.

And a one-night stand, evidently, but she didn't wish that undone. He'd made her feel beautiful and desirable for the first time in ages, maybe more than she'd ever felt before.

Just leave it there, she warned herself. Leave it alone. She was happy enough for now. And as she'd learned, the future brought what it would, good and bad alike.

Chapter Eight

Rory helped her clean up the dishes and put leftover pizza away, even though she protested that she was getting paid to do it.

He laughed it off. "I was raised better, I'm not helpless and anyway, you went above and beyond by agreeing to sing on Regina's song."

She stood with a dish towel in hand. "Why did you insist on that?"

He shrugged his shoulder. "I wanted her to feel that it was a professional kind of recording. Special. Because it was."

What a thoughtful man. She hadn't even considered that. "Are you going back to your studio now?"

He glanced up in the direction of Regina's room. "I don't think so. Mind if I play in here?"

"Hey, whose house is it?"

He laughed again. "You're making it yours, too. Besides, there's this thing called courtesy."

She smiled back at him. "I'll bring the coffee. Assuming you don't mind me hanging out. If you do, I'll go back to my rooms."

"I don't mind. Hang out any time. You're not a problem."

She carried coffee into the living room and offered him a mug. He set it on the table nearby and went back to playing quietly, something she'd never heard before. She settled into one of the armchairs. "You're worried about her," she said.

He glanced at her. "Mildly. She's had stomach bugs before and survived. It's probably nothing, but a parent worries a bit anyway, especially when they turn up their nose at a pizza like that."

She wasn't overly familiar with kids, but she guessed he had a point. "I'll go look in on her. You keep playing."

She ran up the stairs, but quietly, and entered Regina's room. The bedside lamp was on, a book had fallen to the floor and the girl slept peacefully. Abby didn't want to disturb her, but took the risk anyway, touching her forehead and cheek lightly. Regina murmured but didn't move.

Back downstairs she told Rory everything appeared all right. "She's sound asleep, a little warm, but that might be from the blankets. She didn't feel hot."

"Thanks. I'll check her a little later."

"She said her mother was going to ship her things."

He stopped playing. "You noticed that omission, too? Yeah, I've been wondering. I hired someone to pack her room. That stuff should have been here a while ago."

Abby didn't even bother to ask aloud why Stella would have stopped the shipment. All part and parcel of this war, she guessed. Some people could be so cruel. Porter and Stella. Maybe they would make a pair.

Rory resumed playing, a new melody. Sometimes he hummed along with it, once again seeming to be reaching for something. Rally appeared, coming to sit beside the piano. Then the funniest thing happened. When Rory started humming with the music, the dog put back his head and howled. Rory stopped, the dog stopped and then as soon as he started again, the dog howled, too.

Rory stopped playing. "When did you turn musical, boy?"

Rally grinned and wagged his tail in answer.

"You silly dog," said the man, and the next thing Abby knew, the two of them were rolling on the floor together, sort of wrestling and just generally having fun together. Each time Rory stopped, the dog leaped up, then gave a play bow, with wagging tail. He was rewarded with rough-and-tumble kneading and more wrestling, until finally Rory sat up, laughing quietly.

"Uncle," Rory said. "You wore me out. Now tell me how I'm going to write music with you around?"

Rally simply panted and wagged his tail harder.

"I guess you've been missing your runs with Regina," he said, petting the dog. "Pent-up energy. Come on, I'll take you out."

Rory didn't come back for a while, and Abby presumed he was giving the dog a good workout. Finally she decided it was getting late enough to head to bed.

As she passed the foot of the stairs, she heard a cry.

Regina! She raced upstairs and found the girl curled on her side in the bed. She flipped on the overhead light.

"What's wrong?"

"Something inside me popped. It hurts!"

"Where?" Abby asked as she pulled down the blankets. Regina's hand drifted to her lower abdomen.

Then she went to press her hand to Regina's forehead. It was hot, but she noticed something far more worrying. The girl was as white as paste.

"Stay here, I'm getting your dad."

Rory hit hyperdrive when he heard Abby calling him. There was no mistaking the urgency of her cry. He'd taken Rally for a long run but was nearly back and he covered the last few hundred yards at a speed that risked his neck, given the slippery snow and ice on the ground.

"What?" he demanded as he pounded the last few feet on the way to the porch.

"Regina. Something's seriously wrong."

He didn't care that he carried snow on his boots into the house. At least he didn't skid because of the grip on the soles of his hiking boots. He went up the stairs in record time and found his daughter sitting on the edge of her bed.

"Regina?"

"Something popped down here," she said and pointed. "It doesn't hurt as bad now."

But one look at her face told him this was nothing to be dismissed.

"She's gray," Abby said from behind him.

"Yeah. Sweetie, we're going to the hospital. Let me wrap you in blankets."

"I can walk."

Rory hesitated, then decided she could make it down the stairs more safely if he helped her than if he carried her.

Half bent over, Regina pushed her feet into her slippers. Rory grabbed her comforter and passed it to Abby. Then, holding on to the girl tightly so she wouldn't fall, he guided her down the stairs. His heart was thudding, and worry goaded him almost to madness. If anything happened to Regina...

He got his daughter to a chair near the front door. "Stay with her," he asked Abby. "I'm bringing the truck around."

Abby looked back at him from eyes filled with worry.

Wondering what he might meet on the roads, wondering if he should call the air ambulance instead, he did wild calculations in his head.

He was three steps off the porch when he turned around and went back in. Abby looked at him in astonishment.

"This can't wait," he said, and grabbed the phone. He dialed emergency and told them the situation. An understanding woman promised the helicopter would be there in a few minutes, assured him he'd made the right decision.

"The roads are still iced in places," she said. "You wouldn't want to go into a ditch."

"No," he agreed, watching Regina. "Is there anything I should do? She looks so pale."

"Get her to lie down if she can. Take her temperature. If it's over 104, try an ice pack on her neck. We'll be there in fifteen, twenty minutes outside."

Rory hung up. "Thermometer?" he asked. This was his own damn house and he didn't know if he had a thermometer. God, he'd never felt so helpless.

"I have one," said Abby. She disappeared down the hallway at a run and returned in about thirty seconds flat with a digital thermometer. Rory was already encouraging Regina to lie on the couch.

"Dad, it's not that bad."

"Please, honey." He'd never seen anyone look as gray as his daughter did right then. All the color was gone, and her eyes were glassy.

She stood, but still bent over at the middle and he guided her to the couch. "Really, it doesn't hurt quite as bad as when it popped."

Somehow that didn't reassure him. Once Regina was lying on her side, he took the thermometer from Abby and said, "Under the tongue. You remember."

He glanced at Abby who looked almost as pale as his daughter. "How long?"

"It's fast. Just a minute."

He waited impatiently, his gaze fixed on his daughter. His heart throbbed with fear and impatience. His ears strained for the sound of rotors. Holding her hand gently, he stroked her hair.

She spoke when he pulled the thermometer from her mouth. "I'll be okay, Dad. It's probably nothing."

He doubted it, but felt a surge of relief when he read the numbers on the display. "One-oh-one. Of course you're going to be okay. The doctors will make sure of it."

"Yeah, well, I want a pony for this," she said.

Rory managed a smile. "We'll talk about that when you're not holding a sword over my head." He didn't miss how weak Regina's answering smile was. Her eyes closed.

"Regina, stay with me. Please."

She opened her eyes. "I'm really tired. It hurts."

"I know, sweetie." Bending closer he kissed her forehead, hating the heat he felt there. "But you can sleep when the helicopter gets here."

"Helicopter? Cool…" Then she groaned.

"Is it getting worse?"

"Just a little."

Rory could barely stand it. He wanted to rage at the heavens, shake his fist at empty air. His little girl was sick and he squatted here, unable to do a damn thing for her.

A soft hand gripped his shoulder. Abby. He glanced up and read the worry there again. She was feeling it, too. Reaching up his free hand, he covered Abby's with it, while still hanging on to Regina.

"They'll be here any minute," she said. He was sure she meant to be reassuring, but he heard a prayer instead. He had prayers of his own running around inside his head, broken, incoherent slices. But he didn't want to scare Regina, so he forced a superficial calm on himself.

An eternity later, he heard the unmistakable sound of helicopter rotors.

"I'll go out front and meet them," Abby said.

"Thanks." He squeezed Regina's hand and her eyes

opened. "Your ride's almost here," he said cheerfully. "You don't want to miss this."

"No…" But no weak smile answered him this time. With each moment, he felt his daughter slipping away.

Abby watched as the EMTs loaded Regina into the chopper. They made room for Rory, too, and her last view was of a man who looked nearly as pale as his daughter.

She knew she couldn't go with them. She wasn't family. Then there was the dog. He'd changed from the happy overgrown puppy who'd been wrestling with Rory to a seriously worried animal who was pacing restlessly and whining from time to time. She wondered how much he knew.

Having nothing else to do, she filled his water bowl and waited. Rally hunkered close to her, as if seeking comfort, and she kept one hand on his neck, massaging him as she held the phone in her other hand.

Time crept by so slowly it seemed almost not to move at all. She knew what hell was then. She thought Porter had taught her, but now she knew that man, all that pain, didn't come close to what she feared and felt right now.

Rory had promised to call as soon as he knew something, but that might be hours. She could only grip the phone and the dog, and cling. Regina was young, healthy. Whatever this was, she'd recover. They'd figure it out. She had to believe that.

But she kept hearing the girl say, "Something popped." Popped hard enough to make her shriek. That was no gas bubble. Worse, she'd been feeling off since this morning. Whatever had caused that pain had been working on her to the point she hadn't even been able to eat more than a bite of the pizza she was so proud of.

Not good. Not good at all.

Rally laid his huge head on her knee. She hardly noticed and didn't care when he drooled on her jeans. "Poor boy," she said. Poor everyone.

Anxiety crawled through her until she wanted to scream or climb out of her own skin. What was taking so long?

But she knew. The flight, the hospital admission, testing…it could take hours. She didn't know if she could survive hours.

It was nearly eleven, and she looked down at the dog wondering if he could make it the night. Well, of course he could, but he clearly knew something was wrong. How could she leave him? But how could she just sit here worrying about Regina and Rory?

Torn, she made her way through some more minutes. Not family, she reminded herself. She'd be useless at the hospital. They probably wouldn't even let her see Regina.

When the phone finally rang, she was so tense she jumped. Rally stood, his tail wagging just a bit, as if he knew this was important.

She punched the button and moments later Rory's tense voice poured into her ear. "God, she's sick, Abby. They're not sure yet, but she's getting worse fast."

Abby's heart slammed and she sucked desperately for air as the nightmare closed in. "They don't know?" she repeated.

"Not yet. They've taken her for some kind of scan. I called Stella, to let her know."

Abby's stomach sank. "Is she coming?"

"Are you kidding? She says it'll all be over before she can get here, so she'll wait to hear."

"Did...do... Does anyone want her?" It sounded crass even in the midst of her growing terror. Rory didn't seem to care.

"Regina hasn't asked for her. And no, I don't want Stella. I just can't believe..." He paused. "Guess I'm not making sense. She ought to want to be here. She doesn't. End of subject."

"I want to be there," Abby said. "I want desperately to be there. Can I come?"

"If you think you can handle it. Regina's really sick, and she's in and out. I don't know how much of it is the morphine and how much is..." His voice cracked. "If you come be careful on the road. I couldn't handle it if you..."

"I get it," she said. She could tell how hard it was for him to think about anything except his daughter. "Will Rally be okay?" She really wasn't sure about that.

"Give him Regina's blanket. He'll hold till morning."

Indeed, as soon as she put the blanket on the floor, Rally curled up on it. Regina's scent. She made sure he had plenty of water and some food, quickly changed into fresh jeans and a heavy sweater, then set out into the frigid, dark night.

The roads were bad, slick with ice in places. She forced herself to ignore her heart's urgings and drive carefully. It was only fifteen miles to town, but it didn't surprise her that the distance seemed to have grown. Why not? Minutes were now lasting hours, it seemed.

Memorial Hospital's lights were a welcome sight. She found a parking place near the emergency entrance and hurried inside. Ice everywhere. Damn.

Once inside, the reception desk didn't give her any problem. "I'm here for Regina McLane," she told a woman she thought she knew but couldn't place in the stress of the moment. "Abby Jason."

"Yes, Mr. McLane said you were coming. Head straight back, make a right and you'll find him on the left."

She hurried back, avoiding carts and scurrying people, and spied Rory through an open door. He was sitting on a plastic chair beside an open curtain, on the other side of which was an empty gurney. There was a big space, empty now, a space he was staring at. They must have taken Regina somewhere else.

"Rory?"

He looked up. She was shocked by how careworn he looked. He appeared to have aged ten years. "Thanks for coming."

She went straight to him and bent over to hug him. He raised his arms and wrapped them around her waist. "Regina?" she asked.

"Out for more tests. But it gets worse."

She sagged against the empty gurney. "Worse? How?"

"Icy roads, four-car pile-up. They think Regina's going to need surgery, but all their suites are full of seriously injured people and all the surgeons have their hands full."

Abby thought her legs might give way. She gripped the edge of the gurney. "Oh, my God."

"They suspect a ruptured appendix. They're making sure. I don't know what then."

For a few seconds the room seemed to spin around Abby. Collecting herself with difficulty, she grabbed the plastic chair from beside the gurney and moved it over to sit next to Rory. Immediately he clasped her hand.

"Thanks for coming. It's more than her mother was willing to do."

She took the bitterness for what it was. Rory was terrified for his daughter, and seeking some other outlet for the tsunami that was drowning him. "She's a long way away."

"Bull," he said succinctly. "She can hire a plane. She could be here in a couple of hours. Call her when it's over?" He swore.

"Maybe she can't handle hospitals."

"Maybe she can't handle anything except what she wants."

Abby ached so badly that she had to fight back tears of anguish. Rory, his daughter… She was overwhelmed by what was happening to them, by the inability to help, by her own concerns for both of them. Everything else that had once loomed so large on her horizon vanished as if it had never been.

They heard wheels and feet in the hall. Soon two people pushed a gurney through the door with Regina on it. She was on an IV. As soon as she reentered the room they hooked her back up to the heart monitor and automatic blood pressure cuff. Rory stood, Abby pushed herself out of the way.

"What…" Rory began.

A nice man in scrubs touched his arm. "I can't tell you anything. A doctor will be in soon. Meanwhile, we'll keep your daughter comfortable."

Just then Regina muttered, "Sick." The subsequent sound was unmistakable. His arm shooting out like a snake, Rory grabbed the front of his daughter's hospital gown and yanked her upright and a little forward as she vomited. There wasn't much, but the retching seemed to go on forever.

Immediately a nurse was there, that same one who had just left them. He wiped the girl's mouth, then the sheet vanished, replaced by a fresh green one. "We're working on getting her bumped up in the surgery queue," he said. "We're working on it. But the auto accident. Surgeons can't pull out in the middle of an operation."

"I get it," Rory said tensely.

"We're hoping to find that one of the accident victims can wait a little while…"

"Okay." The word was clipped, tight.

The nurse paused. "Your daughter may not appear awake, Mr. McLane, but she can hear you. Keep talking to her."

Rory took his daughter's hand. At first he talked about what kind of horse she might want and about the coming holidays, about how beautiful she would make the house for them all. After a while, as if he didn't know what else to say, he started to sing to her.

Abby listened to him, realizing he was singing happy songs, among them the song Regina had written for him. Then some chatter about Rally and how he was looking forward to running with her just as soon as she came home. Then back to singing.

Abby pushed the chair away and stood behind him, rubbing his shoulders, tearing her gaze from Regina occasionally to glance at the monitor. Heartbeat and blood pressure registered there, and as the time crept by, she didn't like that the blood pressure kept falling. Little by little it kept creeping down. She was sure that couldn't be good.

Finally she looked at the wall clock and realized hours had passed. Hours? What the hell? She wanted to go grab a doctor by his throat.

When Rory fell silent briefly, either out of words or too overcome, she leaned over Regina. "I love you," she told the girl in as strong a voice as she could manage. "We're going to cook Thanksgiving dinner together, and decorate the house just as much as you want for Christmas. You like those twinkle lights? I do. And I'll help you with the words to more songs. Do you want me to call Betsy for you? Anybody else?"

It was useless patter. The girl didn't answer. She vomited again, and then she groaned so loudly it was almost a scream. The pain was worsening.

Finally the doctor appeared. His name badge said *Dr. David.* Before speaking to them, he checked the monitor and scanned a computer screen.

Rory was on his feet now, still holding Regina's hand.

Dr. David finally gave them his full attention. "It appears to be a ruptured appendix. If not, it's something very similar. She definitely needs surgery."

"What's going on?" Rory demanded. "She's sinking. I can see it and I'm no doctor."

"Some of that's the morphine," Dr. David answered. "But right now she's got a massive infection working in her. We've started antibiotics intravenously, but she needs to be cleaned out inside."

"How long is that going to be?" Rory's voice held a definite edge.

"Soon. That's all I can say. We've got people in the suites with their chests open. One of our surgeons is moving as fast as he can. We're triaging the other victims to see who can wait." He clapped his hand to Rory's shoulder. "We're doing absolutely everything we can, I promise you."

"Everything," Rory repeated, sounding almost numb as the doctor walked away. "I can't believe this is everything."

Abby didn't know what to do. She couldn't offer any comfort other than stupid palliatives. Regina's breathing was getting shallower. She looked almost sallow now. Her blood pressure was frighteningly low.

All she could do was wrap her arms around Rory and hug him tight. Terror had crept into her heart, as well. She could no longer imagine a life without Regina. Couldn't do it. Love was once again cracking her heart in two.

"It won't be long," said a woman nurse finally. Abby glanced at the clock. God, it was already six in the morning.

The nurse picked up the phone on the wall near the bed and punched in a number. "It's extremely urgent," she said bluntly. "We don't have long. Yes, tell him. All right." Then she hung up.

"Regina is next in line. We're going to take her up there as soon as I get a call."

Then she leaned over Regina. "Regina," she said loudly, "you're next in line. We have a doctor for you. It won't be long. Stay with me. Regina, stay with me!" It was a command. "Open your eyes."

Regina's lids fluttered.

"Good girl," said the nurse, talking so loudly it was almost a shout. "Hang on just a little longer. You're next. Now stay with me."

Listening to the nurse, Abby realized that Regina was at death's door. As she watched Rory, she saw the knowledge in his own eyes. Those blue depths blazed with fear and recognition.

He still held his daughter's hand. Bending over her, he said loudly, "Regina, I love you. Hear me? You better hang on or you'll never get that horse."

Another cry escaped the girl, nearly a shriek. Abby started trembling. All that pain through morphine?

"That's it," said the nurse, still talking at full volume. "You fight it, Regina. Daddy promised you a horse. You're next and we're going to fix you. Stay with me!"

The phone rang and the nurse snatched it. "On the way" was all she said.

She turned to them. "We're clearing the OR. She'll be in the surgeon's hands in ten minutes. You hear that Regina? Just ten more minutes. We're taking you now."

Abby and Rory watched as they took her away. The nurse told them where the surgery waiting room was, and suggested they take a few minutes to grab some coffee or food from the cafeteria.

Rory reached out to her. "Is she...will she?"

The nurse hesitated. "I'm not a doctor."

"Then talk to me as a person. Please."

"She's going to be in excellent hands. Dr. Ted is one of our best, and he just hurried through thoracic surgery for Regina."

"But…"

"I'm sorry, I can't say any more. But if I were you, I'd want my daughter to be going right where Regina's going now."

Sitting in the surgery waiting room was hardly any better, except that now they were sure Regina was getting the treatment she needed. Abby went to get some coffee for them, but Rory refused food and she didn't want any, either.

They sat side by side in basic padded waiting chairs, watching the second hand sweep on the wall clock.

"I'm glad you came," Rory said. "I needed you."

"I haven't done anything."

He turned toward her, his eyes blazing. "You were here. That matters. You give a damn. That matters."

Twisting toward him, she reached out and they hugged one another. "She's going to be all right. I'm sure of it."

"Maybe. Probably." He unleashed a long shaky sigh. "You want to put things in perspective? This'll do it."

She had to agree. All the other things that had troubled her, all the demons that tormented her inside since Porter, seemed like little imps with dull pitchforks now, unable to touch her beyond mere pinpricks.

They broke the hug, then sat with hands twined. "I've made up my mind," he said.

"About what?"

"No more touring until Regina is out of high school. I'm going to stay right here, get her the damn horse, or a dozen if she wants, and raise my girl. There aren't any days to waste."

So obviously true. One of those trite things he talked about that hit home like a ton of bricks. How much of life was wasted by focusing on entirely the wrong things? Worrying about the wrong things? Too much, she thought miserably. Entirely too much.

"I didn't just decide this tonight," he said.

"You mentioned it before."

"Yeah. When I first came out here, I thought it would be temporary. It's a long way from Regina, even though Stella made sure I hardly ever saw her."

Abby's chest tightened. "How did she do that?"

"Well, only certain holidays were written in the final decree. The rest of the time we were supposed to work things out. Stella made sure that Regina had other things to do when I was in town on weekends, sent her away to camp for the summer... What with one thing or another I got to see her only a few times and only for a few hours since Christmas."

"That's awful!" Abby couldn't imagine the pettiness of it, although given what she'd heard about Stella, she wondered why she should be surprised.

"Anyway, then Regina came to stay with me, and I started thinking about how quickly she was growing up and how much I was missing. Tonight just solidified it."

Abby squeezed his hand, waiting, but he said no more. Eventually he freed his hand and put his arm around her shoulders. "Thank you," he said.

"You don't need to thank me. I was scared, too. I wanted to be here."

At long last the surgeon appeared and he was smiling. He shook their hands saying, "She's going to be fine. Her appendix ruptured and spread infection everywhere. We've cleaned it out, and after a couple of days on IV antibiotics, she'll be able to come home. In the meantime, she's in recovery. We should be able to move her to a room in a few hours and then you can see her. And tonight when I check on her I'll answer any of your questions, but I have another surgery waiting right now."

Rory hugged Abby so tightly that she almost squeaked. "Thank God," he whispered. "Thank God."

Then he kissed her, lightly but warmly.

When he released her, Abby felt a huge sense of loss. But then she'd already figured she could stay in those arms forever. Even so, they weren't hers to claim.

She touched his cheek lightly. "Will you be okay now? This would be a good time for me to take care of Rally. I'll be back later to see Regina."

He seized her in another tight hug. "Hurry back," he said roughly. "I'm going to miss you."

Chapter Nine

Regina came home from the hospital two days later. She was still sore and took over the couch downstairs, but she looked so much better it seemed miraculous. Propped on pillows, in a comfy nightgown with an extraordinarily happy dog on the floor beside her, she announced, "Don't let me do that again."

Abby and Rory both laughed. "Like we had anything to say about it," said Rory. "And I think most people have only one appendix."

"And now I have none," Regina said smugly. "I am so special." Then her expression changed. "I really scared you guys, huh?"

"Out of my mind," Rory admitted.

"Me, too," Abby agreed. "And don't forget Rally. That dog was miserable. He knew something was seriously wrong."

Regina stretched out a hand to pat him. He was so big, she didn't have to reach far. "More worried than Mom, probably."

Abby sank internally. Stella's absence was spectacular. Not even a phone call. Rory had called her to let her know what had happened and that had been it.

"Honey," Rory started.

"Don't bother," Regina said. "I had to live with her, remember? I wasn't whining. It's just that the dog loves me more than she does. What more is there?"

Abby felt sick for her. No girl should have to feel that way about her mother, yet in all honesty, there were probably plenty in the world who didn't feel loved.

"Abby cared more," Regina remarked. "And she doesn't even have to."

Abby met Rory's troubled gaze and sought to lighten the moment. "Well, of course I don't have to. You put me under your spell, though, and here I am. Darn it, I love you."

Regina managed a cautious giggle. "My spell, huh? And did I hear something about a horse?"

Rory looked at Abby. "I knew she was pretending the whole time."

That got another smile from Regina. "Well, you kinda shouted it at me. Like that nurse. Stay with her? I can think of better people to stay with. Horse?"

"Yes," said Rory. "Horse. For Christmas. Once we get your mother settled down."

Regina waved a hand. "Oh, that's easy. I know about the cocaine she keeps in her jewelry box."

Regina dozed off early on the couch that evening. Her appetite had improved dramatically, and she even ate a cold piece of her own pizza. But the illness and surgery had left her worn out, and probably would for a while.

When Rory went out to run the dog before bed, Abby went to her own apartment, leaving the door open so she could hear if Regina called out. She curled up on the rocker in a fresh pair of sweats, wondering why the room felt chilly tonight, deciding it must be her. She was worn out from the last couple of days, too, and not even seeing Regina's remarkably speedy improvement could undo it all.

The phone rang just as Rory and the dog returned and she let him answer it.

She had other things to think about, such as how fond she had become of Regina. Almost without noticing it, she had come to love Rory's daughter and couldn't imagine life without her. If she'd needed any proof, the last few days had given it to her.

Then there was Rory. All her distrust had evaporated. Anyone would be lucky to have that man's love. But she couldn't escape the feeling that she was living in a temporary situation, that sooner or later she'd need to move on for some reason. Even if she postponed all thought of going back to school, there'd come a day when Rory would decide to go back to Nashville, or when he'd meet another woman and want to get married. She doubted she'd be welcome as a housekeeper then.

But mostly she thought about Regina's shocking revelation earlier. Rory had been furious. He hadn't blown up, or even raised his voice, but the edge in his words as he asked Regina how she knew that had been unmistakable. It had only gotten worse when

Regina had blithely said, "There's other stuff, too. But I'm tired."

Rory had left the room to make a call, and she presumed it was to his lawyer, but she didn't know. The rest of the day had continued quietly, as if a huge bomb hadn't been dropped.

No girl that age should be exposed to that, Abby thought with horrified anger. No parent should expose their child to that. *Cocaine?* Her opinion of Stella had been low before, but now the woman had relocated to the subbasement in Abby's estimation. She wasn't totally naive. She knew some folks liked drugs. Some of her friends had smoked marijuana back in their high school and college days. But to do it around your kid?

And what if the child decided to try it? Abby shuddered at the risks.

A knock on her doorframe alerted her. She looked up and smiled, waving Rory to come in. He perched on the couch as always, elbows on his knees. He still looked tired, too, and while he'd cleaned up earlier, going out to run with dog had left him looking a bit rumpled. His shirt was half-untucked and his hair was ruffled.

"That was my lawyer," he said without preamble.

"I figured you'd called him earlier. Can I say I'm still in shock?"

"You're not the only one. I lived with that woman and I didn't think she was *that* careless or stupid."

Abby just shook her head. She seemed to be running out of emotions. Maybe she was stuck in some kind of shell shock after all of this. "Dangerous" was the only word she could utter. "Was your lawyer helpful?"

"He said—" He broke off as the phone rang. "Damn, how is that girl going to rest?"

"Here." Abby passed him her extension.

He looked at the caller ID. "Stella." For a second he looked as if he wouldn't answer, then his face changed drastically. "Regina picked it up."

He took off like a shot, and Abby wasn't far behind him. They both arrived in the living room in time to hear Regina say, "My home is here now, Mom. Sorry if you don't like it. If you try to take me away again, I'll tell a judge about your cocaine. About how you fired one of my nannies because she got into your stash." A minute of silence. "Did you think I was deaf, dumb and blind because I was a kid? Well, I wasn't. So don't try to take me away."

Then Regina punched the off button and sagged. Rory went to her instantly, taking the phone from her limp hand. "I'm sorry I didn't get it first."

Regina's eyes popped open. "I'm not. I needed to say it."

He perched next to her on the couch. "You didn't have to get in the middle. My lawyer was handling it. Oh, God, sweetie, I didn't want you in the middle. You're too young."

"Which is why I wound up with her last time. Well, I'm not going back, and I'm not too young to know who's good for me. Just do me one favor?"

"What's that?"

"Let me sleep. And make Abby my stepmother for Christmas." Then she dozed off again.

Silence filled the room like concrete. Almost unable to breathe, Abby hurried down the hall to her bedroom. Once there, she closed it, leaned back against it and wondered what she was supposed to do now.

Any line-crossing they'd been worried about had just been utterly and completely crossed, putting Rory on the spot in a terrible way. She doubted she'd be able to look him in the eye again for a long time.

The worst of it was, Regina had just voiced the deepest of her desires, one she had been hiding from herself.

She wished the earth would open and swallow her.

Some time later, she heard a knock on her door. She was still leaning against it, and felt it almost as much as she heard it. Rory, being quiet in case she was sleeping.

She desperately wanted to pretend to be asleep, but she was realistic enough to know that postponing this conversation wasn't going to make anything any easier.

She gathered her courage, feeling like a warrior facing combat for the first time, and opened the door.

Rory stood there, still disheveled from his run with the dog. "She sure threw the tinder on that fire," he said quietly.

"What fire?" Pretending to be obtuse seemed like her only option.

He smiled crookedly. "She ruined all my plans. Am I allowed in?"

Finally she stepped back and waved him in. The door remained open a few inches, and to her surprise Rally nosed his way in. When she sat on her rocker, he collapsed at her side. Rory once again took the couch. This scene was becoming all too familiar.

She craved this man, she realized. Out of all reason, against all instinct, she craved him. She knew better than to risk her heart again, but she had already risked it. All that remained was the inevitable anguish. She supposed she deserved it for being so foolish.

"I had plans," he said finally. "They did *not* involve my daughter proposing on my behalf."

She wet her lips. Her mouth had gone dry as sand. "I'm sure. Just ignore it." As if either of them could. But maybe they could pretend.

"I can't." He looked rueful. "I was planning… I was thinking…" He sighed. "Oh, heck. I hoped that you were coming to trust me and love me. At Christmas I intended to do the bended knee and roses thing, offer you a ring and pray that you'd say yes."

Shock exploded in her. "You *what*?"

"See?" His smile faded. "You're still recovering from Porter. I can't imagine how hard it's going to be for you to trust a man again. I figured maybe in time you might trust me. But maybe not. Like you said, we've both got hot buttons. Chances are I'd do some fool thing that would utterly convince you I'm a jerk."

"Rory…" Her heart was swelling until it felt as if it would burst from her chest.

"But maybe it's not totally blown. Unless you're scared out of your mind now, do you think you could hang around and give me a chance?"

Give him a chance? She reran the words in her mind, wondering if she was misunderstanding. But no, they seemed clear. As long as her hearing wasn't being affected by wishful thinking. "Um…I hope you're not saying these things because of Regina."

He shook his head. "She kind of forced my hand.

But I wouldn't marry anyone just because Regina wanted it. Just as I wouldn't marry anyone she hated. She's part of the decision, but this is between you and me. I come with a daughter attached. Her feelings count, but they aren't the deciding factor unless she hates someone. Did I make that clear? I feel like I'm wandering here."

"You are," she admitted. "You know I love Regina."

"Yeah, I do." His words were emphatic. "For that reason alone, I want you to know you can stay here as long as you want, no strings. She's attached to you. I'd never try to break that. But, big but, I'm attached to her. And I'd kind of like it if this was a package deal."

Uncertainty was building in her again. Package deal? What kind of package deal? Had she misunderstood him when he talked about marriage?

She closed her eyes a moment, her hands clenching. She wanted to leap across the space between them and feel his strong arms around her, but that would only make matters muddier right now. "Rory..." She opened her eyes. "What's a package deal?"

His eyes widened a shade, then he astonished her by laughing.

"Lousy word choice," he said. "Okay. Let me be perfectly clear."

"Please. In so many words."

He smiled, rose and came to kneel before her, taking her hands in his. "Abby, I love you. I fell in love with you before I even realized it, but I know it now to the deepest part of my soul. I want you in my life forever, I want you to be my bride, my wife and maybe mother to some future kids. I want to grow old with you at my side, and we'll sit on a front porch swing and I'll play and sing for you as the sun begins to set. Forever."

She felt tears moisten her eyes, and one escaped, running down her cheek. Joy filled her until she grew certain she couldn't contain it. "You know that homesickness we talked about, that thing you long for and can't quite remember?"

He nodded.

"I found it with you. I'm not homesick for something I can't remember anymore. I'm homesick for you."

She fell forward into his arms then, and, kneeling on the floor, they embraced tightly. He kissed her deeply, unleashing all the hunger and need and caring they felt.

"I love you," he said again. "Love you."

"I love you, too," she answered, burying her face in his shoulder. "Ah, Rory, I love you so much."

Just then, Rally shoved his head between them, pushing them apart. Rory fell back on his hands, and Abby caught herself on the edge of the rocker.

"Hey," said Rory. "I was hugging my lady here."

The dog gave them each a sloppy kiss before sitting down and grinning at them.

Abby looked at Rory and they both burst into laughter. "I guess he was feeling left out," Rory said. Then he pulled Abby into his arms again and lifted her to the pinnacle of happiness.

Epilogue

Rory and Abby married in a quiet ceremony at home two days before Christmas, giving Regina her wish. Regina had gone to town with the Christmas theme, and the living room was filled with a huge decorated tree, sparkling white lights and big red velvet bows. Dozens of poinsettias lined the room. The scent of pine perfumed the air.

Their parents attended as did some of their friends, but it wasn't a large gathering. Regina had written another song for the occasion, this time with Rory's help, and unsurprisingly it held the words, "The sun rises and sets in your eyes."

Stella had dropped her custody battle quickly and attempted to play the martyred mother, but that story didn't sell well, so she began to say that she had chosen to give her daughter a more stable life with her father, who had given up touring.

He had, too. For at least eight years. He promised both Abby and Regina that he would always be here with them.

He'd also done some remarkable things for Abby's parents. Her mom no longer needed to work, and they now lived in Abby's old apartment in the back of the house, once again among family and their old lifelong friends. Rory's parents were returning to their home in Jamaica after New Year's, and promises of many future visits had flown in both directions.

But all of that faded into the background as Abby, in a simple white dress adorned with a big red bow, eased around a Great Dane and crossed the living room to stand in front of the minister with Rory. One look in his smiling blue eyes, and nothing else existed.

She was where she had always belonged, with the man she had waited her whole life for, and as Regina's flute-like voice faded along with the piano on the last notes of the song, she felt her heart take wing.

The journey had begun.

* * * * *

1015_MB515

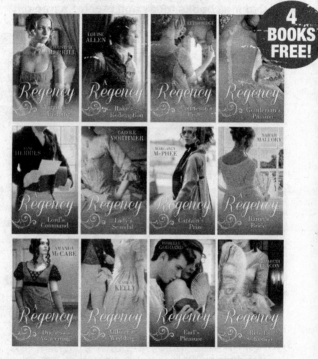
0915_ST19

MILLS & BOON®

Cherish™

EXPERIENCE THE ULTIMATE RUSH OF FALLING IN LOVE